Lizzie's Worst Year

THIS BOOK

Anne Foley

BELONGS TO

Look for these and
other Apple Paperbacks
in your local bookstore!

Dear Dad, Love Laurie
by Susan Beth Pfeffer

Leah's Song
(Original title: *The Man Who Sang in the Dark*)
by Eth Clifford

Sixth Grade Secrets
by Louis Sachar

Turning Thirteen
by Susan Beth Pfeffer

A Ghost in the Window
by Betty Ren Wright

A Secret Friend
by Marilyn Sachs

Lizzie's Worst Year

Catherine Robinson

Illustrated by Liz Roberts

AN
APPLE
PAPERBACK

SCHOLASTIC INC.
New York Toronto London Auckland Sydney

To Chloë
with love

Original title: *Lizzie Oliver*

No part of this publication may be reproduced in whole or in part, or stored in a retrieval system, or transmitted in any form or by any means, electronic, mechanical, photocopying, recording, or otherwise, without written permission of the publisher. For information regarding permission, write to Macdonald Children's Books, Simon and Schuster International Group, Wolsey House, Wolsey Road, Hemel Hempstead, Hertfordshire HP2 4SS, England.

ISBN 0-590-43120-x

12 11 10 9 8 7 6 5 4 3 2 1   0 1 2 3 4 5/9
Printed in the U.S.A.   40
First Scholastic Printing March 1990

CONTENTS

PART ONE
Cornwall

Penwithin   9
The Birthday Party   18
Maudie   29
Ben writes a Letter   36
Getting ready for Christmas   43
Christmas at the Vicarage   48
I get a Shock   57
An awful New Year   62
My thirteenth Birthday   73
The Wedding   85

PART TWO
London

Barnes   101
Oaklands and Amber   110
Pippa befriends me   121
The Liver Incident   132
Jacob and Emma   141
Back to Penwithin   152
Disaster for Rufus   163
Taken ill   174
The last Straw!   183
An End – and a new Beginning   192

PART ONE
Cornwall

1

Penwithin

The seagull seemed to be suspended in the air, silhouetted against the clear blue of the late summer sky. Daddy says that seagulls "ride the thermals" - I always thought that thermals were the long underwear you wore in winter, to keep the cold out. I suppose Daddy knows what he's on about.

I rolled over on to my front and took another bite out of my apple. The sun felt good on the back of my neck. I started to think about school tomorrow - that didn't feel so good. The trouble with the summer holidays is that they always have to end, and the end of the summer holidays always seems to come at the beginning of the decent weather. When I'm Prime Minister, I thought, crunching the apple, I'll make the summer holidays last for ages and ages - until about the middle of October. That should just about be long enough. And while I'm at it, I'll make it a rule that schoolchildren need only study those subjects that interest them.

I'm not that good at school. It's a bit embarrassing really because Daddy writes educational books, so you'd think I'd be clever like him. But I'm not. The only thing

I'm good at is music; at least, everybody else seems to think I'm good at music. I just know I enjoy it.

Something else Daddy does (when he's not writing educational books) is write poetry. He's started to sell some of it, too, which pleases him, because he says it's the jam which goes on the bread and butter. The educational books are the bread and butter. I think other people must think the jam pretty good: the other week I was in the Polkerris' shop and I heard a lady with a very posh accent say to Mrs Polkerris, "Not *the* James Oliver?", looking at me curiously. I don't think of my father as *the* James Oliver, or even *a* James Oliver – he's just Daddy. I think these tourists can be so rude; grockles, Daddy calls them.

Anyway, I digress, as they say in books. The reason I was mentioning the poetry is that Daddy says he gets the inspiration to write it by the beautiful Cornish countryside here at Penwithin where we live. I know what he means. Sitting on the clifftop – as I was doing then – listening to the seagulls, watching the foamy Atlantic waves break over the grey rocks below, tasting the salty spray on my lips – I could always feel something stir deep within me. For Daddy, it came out as poetry. For me, it was when I played my violin that I most felt it.

I finished my apple and tossed the core to a seagull, who swooped on it immediately. Then I took out the bag of bread I'd brought and began throwing bits to the gulls, tossing it up into the air. I loved watching them swoop down on the bread, catching it unerringly in their beaks. The biggest seagulls in Britain were supposed to live in this particular part of North Cornwall. I'm not surprised – the amount of bread I fed them.

Rufus came crashing through the broom, plumy tail

waving. He's got this peculiar radar which always homes in on any food that's going, even stale bread. He thinks he's a seagull, not a golden retriever. I threw him a couple of bits which he gobbled down as though they were rump steak. Stupid dog. If I'd put them in his food bowl he'd have ignored them disdainfully.

"Stupid dog!" I said. He grinned at me. He knew I loved him really.

Just then, I heard someone call my name. I saw a familiar figure in a red jersey coming up the steep cliff path.

"Hi, Lizzie!" he shouted again. I waved to him.

"Ben! What are you doing here?"

"I thought I'd find you up here," he said. He reached the top of the path and flopped down beside me. "I've made a card in honour of your Dad's birthday. I wanted to read the verse to you before the party, to see what you think of it." He removed his jersey and tied it around his waist. "Phew – it's hot!"

Ben Polkerris is my best friend. Girls at school think it's funny that my best friend is a boy – but he doesn't seem like a boy. By that I mean he never teases or torments me, or goes on about being bigger and stronger and older than me, which lots of boys tend to do with girls. Or cleverer, which he undoubtedly is. He never brags or boasts, despite the fact that he won a scholarship when he was quite young, and was away at school in Devon. Well, not at that precise moment – he was home for the summer holidays – but he was going back next week. He wasn't much looking forward to it, I knew – he'd told me he hadn't made many friends there. All the same his holidays were a week longer than mine: *I* was going back to school tomorrow, but I go to the comprehensive school in the next village. I should hate to go to a boarding school and have to live away from home.

"Come on then," I said, sitting up and selecting a juicy grass to chew. "Let's see this wonderful card." Ben started to read it.

"I wrote this poem just to say
I hope you have a lovely day.
I know you won't think me a smartie
When I say 'Enjoy your party!'
Lizzie's made a cake for you:
There's lots of other nice things, too.
We'll all be pleased to drink your health
And wish you luck, and love, and wealth.
In short, you should have lots of fun
Now that you are forty-one."

He looked expectantly at me: "Well – what d'you think?"

"It's great," I said. "There's – er – just one thing wrong with it."

"What's that?" asked Ben.

"He's forty," I said, "not forty-one. I don't think he'd be awfully pleased if you added an extra year on."

"Oh blast," said Ben with feeling. He tore the page with the poem on in two, before I could stop him, and let the pieces flutter in the breeze over the cliff.

"What did you do that for?" I asked him in dismay. "Couldn't you just have changed the last two lines?"

"No," said Ben. "It would've been OK if he was a year younger – I could have said 'I hope that life treats you just fine, now that you are thirty-nine,' or something. But what rhymes with forty?"

I pondered awhile.

"Shortie?" I suggested.

"Oh, great," he said, his voice heavy with sarcasm. "I can just hear it – 'Lizzie is a little shortie, now you've reached the age of forty'!" His voice rose squeakily at the end of the sentence – it had been doing that a lot lately. It sounded like my violin did if I drew the bow over the string and moved my finger up it swiftly. But I didn't say anything about it. Ben had grown self-conscious about his voice and didn't thank people for drawing attention to it.

"Never mind," I comforted him instead. "It was a nice thought."

"Yes," he agreed, "but the poem was pretty hopeless, wasn't it? Frightful doggerel, really. I can't seem to write anything good."

I know that not being able to write is the bane of Ben's life. He's very artistic – he likes reading, he paints beautiful pictures, and he's the only boy of my age I know who appreciates my music.

Thinking about it, I suppose that's why we get on so well together. We've both got talents – gifts, I suppose – that we have to use or they'll wither and die. It sounds dramatic, I know. But that's how it is.

"Why don't you try and do something for Christmas?" I suggested. "When you're back at school – you'll have plenty of time then."

"Huh," said Ben, sitting up and hugging his knees. "I'll be lucky, what with all the games and things we've got to do. The Head's always banging on about what an honour it is to be picked to play for the school. I couldn't care less."

I sympathised. "It's a shame you're not musical," I said. "After my first term at school last year, I was allowed to skip games. Well, actually, I forged a letter from Daddy saying he was afraid I'd damage my hands, playing hockey or something, and ruin my violin playing."

"Did they fall for it?" Ben asked, looking interested.

"Yes, but the only problem is, they decided I should do extra music practice instead. So I'm stuck in a practice room on my own. And I *have* to practise, or they'll hear me – or rather, they won't, and they'll know I'm skiving." I sighed.

Ben laughed. "Serves you right! But at least it gets you out of games."

"What are you getting for your birthday?" I asked, changing the subject. He was fourteen next week – the day after he went back to Devon. I remembered the first birthday I'd had after the Awful Time – my eleventh. I pushed the thought to the back of my mind. "What are you getting?" I repeated.

"A cricket bat," he said, unhappily. "That's what Mum and Dad think fourteen-year-old boys want for their birthdays." Mr and Mrs Polkerris run the Post Office-cum-General Store in the village – a treasure trove full of goodies.

"Crikey!" Ben said suddenly, sitting up. "I've just remembered – I've forgotten something!"

I was intrigued.

"How on earth can you remember you've forgotten something?"

"You know what I mean, clever-clogs. I've forgotten to buy your Dad a birthday present."

"Oh, that's all right," I said. "He won't expect you to get him a present. Just come to the party."

"But I must get him something. It's really rude to go to somebody's birthday party without a present." He looked at his watch. It was half-past three. "What time did you say to come?"

"About five," I said, my eyes closed. He stood up and threw his jersey around his shoulders.

"See you later then – don't fall asleep and get sunstroke, or you won't be able to eat any birthday cake!" he shouted as he ran down the path. Rufus bounded after him, barking, thinking it was a huge game.

"Mind you wash behind your ears!" I yelled as a parting shot. "Rufus, come here!" He slunk back, hangdog. "Now lie down here and guard me." He'd make a rotten guard-dog; he'd smother everyone with love.

I was looking forward to the birthday cake – I'd made it myself and Mrs Morris had helped me to ice it. White, with a big blue '40' on the top. "Blue for a boy," Mrs Morris had said. She came from Birmingham, and comes in every day except Sunday to help me look after Daddy. (I don't mean she comes in from Birmingham every day – she lives locally now.)

I didn't think 'blue for a boy' was very apt – after all, forty is hardly a boy. When you're forty you're ancient. I don't like to think of Daddy as ancient, although he'd got rather grey lately. He said it was due to working hard. The grey hairs had started to appear about the same time as the Awful Time, and he'd got greyer since.

I fondled Rufus' ears. "You'd like some birthday cake, wouldn't you?" Stupid question. He'd polish the lot off, given half the chance. He's a great advertisement for my cooking, not being fussy about his food. Daddy says he's a stomach on legs.

My cooking isn't terribly good, I have to confess. But it is improving. It has to really – it can't get any worse, and I get enough practice. Ben says I make the best scrambled eggs and Welsh Rarebit he's ever tasted – but then, he's a bit like Rufus when it comes to food. He eats things like kipper and marmalade sandwiches – gross. No wonder his voice has gone squeaky.

Daddy tries to enjoy my cooking, and sometimes he succeeds. Compared to his efforts, it's brilliant: his idea of food is a Mars bar every so often.

I suppose I'd better explain about the Awful Time. I mean, I expect it sounds odd, me doing all this cooking and everything. And Mrs Morris coming in to help out. And I know I go on about Daddy rather a lot - that's because I worry about him a bit. When he's writing, he forgets about normal things, like eating and sleeping. So I have to sort of prod him into action every so often. I also go on about him because most children have two parents, but I've only got him, so he's got to have twice as much love and care and things like that. It's not all sloppy stuff though - he gets twice as much shouting and rows too. We don't get on brilliantly *all* the time - I have to keep him on his toes.

But I'm digressing again. The Awful Time: I call it that because it *was* awful, and somehow it's easier to call it that than anything else. Daddy doesn't call it anything at all - we never discuss it. Nearly two years before (ages previously really - I was only ten), on Christmas Eve my mother died in a car crash. She skidded on some ice when she was coming back with the Christmas tree. It was horrible, and I don't want to write about what happened.

Most of the time I feel almost over it. I sometimes think I've forgotten what she looks like (and, in a way, that's the worst thing of all), but then my little niece Katey smiles, and something about her twinkling eyes makes me think of my mother. It's ridiculous - Katey's only six months old - but there you are. When it happens, bits of my inside seem to move about with a great heave and end up in my throat.

Daddy locked away, or threw away, all my mother's

photographs, except one, which he keeps in his bedroom. She was a painter. We sometimes see pictures by her in shops in other bits of Cornwall, which is a bit hard on Daddy. But he usually walks past without seeing them.

I threw my arms around Rufus, feeling sad. He's not very sensitive to moods and rolled around on his back, lolling his tongue and wagging his feathery tail. I threw a stick for him and he chased after it, ever-eager for a game. It made me feel better. We chased around, Rufus bellowing at the gulls, who floated in a superior fashion on their thermals and ignored him. I looked at my watch. Quarter to five. Enough time to get back to the cottage and change into my posh frock before people started arriving for Daddy's birthday party.

I walked down the cliff path, whistling to Rufus who was sniffing for rabbits. My sad mood had gone. I stopped on the crest of the hill and looked at the harbour, spread before me below. It was low tide and little brightly-painted fishing boats were drawn up to the Platt. White-painted cottages clustered around the harbour, like old women gossiping, and spread up along the hill opposite me. I could see the lifeboat men in their bright yellow oilskins, dots in the distance, going for their weekly practice. They'd have to push the lifeboat out a long way this evening, I thought, before they could launch it.

My 'Cornish cliffs' feeling swept over me. I loved it here. I could never live anywhere else. It was home.

Calling Rufus, I swung home to the party.

2

The Birthday Party

The first thing I noticed when I let myself into the cottage was that it was unusually quiet. The second thing was that it was unusually tidy. Miss Bullock must have been in, tidying up, I thought – Mrs Morris' idea of tidying up was to leave everything where it was and clean up around it. She was afraid of losing things belonging to Daddy: "mustn't upset the genius at work," she would say. I think she was being sarcastic.

Miss Bullock never worried about upsetting the genius. She swooped in, like the gulls on the bread, collecting up papers, notebooks, learned articles, spectacles, empty coffee cups, the lot – terrifying to watch. I always thought that, if Daddy or I were unlucky enough to get in the way, we'd have been swooped up too.

Miss Bullock is Daddy's friend – girlfriend, I suppose, though I don't really like the idea much. For one thing, she's years younger than him. She's a teacher at the local primary school – I think that must be why she's so good at organizing. She sometimes forgets Daddy's age and treats him like one of her nine-year-olds, but he doesn't seem to mind.

A shaft of the late afternoon sunlight was coming through the kitchen window. Fishpaste was sitting on the pine dresser in the pool of sun, washing his whiskers. Fishpaste is my cat; I mean, really mine. Rufus is officially Daddy's dog, but he loves everybody. Daddy gave me Fishpaste – a tiny bundle of ginger and white fur – on my eleventh birthday. It was the first one after the Awful Time, and Daddy thought a kitten would be a nice present for me. He was right, although Fishpaste is hardly a tiny kitten any more. He's huge – he's got the same sort of appetite as Rufus and Ben.

It really was awfully quiet. I could hear the slow tick of the clock on the dresser and see the mites of dust swirling in the patch of sunlight. There was a new red geranium in a copper pot on the windowsill – Miss Bullock *has* been busy, I thought. Fishpaste started to wash his ears.

"Daddy!" I called. "Where are you? I'm home!" A muffled voice came from upstairs. "Up here, sweetie. Come and talk to me!"

He was in the bathroom, shaving. That explained the quiet – Daddy has to concentrate on shaving. On more than one occasion, a brilliant idea had occurred to him in the middle and he'd gone wandering into his study in his vest with half his face still covered in foam. I sat on the edge of the bath and swung my legs.

"The kitchen looks nice," I remarked.

"Doesn't it, though," agreed Daddy, negotiating a particularly stubborn bit under his chin. "Wendy's been in, making the place look respectable for this evening. I thought it looked respectable enough before, but I must admit it looks better now."

I thought as much. I could recognise Miss Bullock's 'feminine little touches' anywhere.

"I'd better get changed," I said. "They'll all be here in a minute."

Before I changed, though, I went quietly downstairs. I took something out of one of the dresser drawers. It was a paper streamer, with 'Happy 40th Birthday to my Dear Daddy' written on it. I'd made it myself. I was quite pleased with it, even though I'd run out of space towards the end of the lettering, and the last 'dy' of 'Daddy' was squashed up a bit.

I stuck it up across the wall with sticky tape. Then I took the cake out of the pantry and put it on the table. Rufus appeared, wagging hopefully, his radar switched on as usual. I had second thoughts, and put the cake back. Meg could help me when she arrived.

When I got back upstairs, Daddy was in his bedroom, getting changed. I could hear him humming to himself and smell the tang of his aftershave.

"You're not allowed to go downstairs until we tell you it's OK," I called through his bedroom door.

"Why ever not?" he asked.

"Because you're not!"

He chuckled. "Fair enough. Don't forget to wash your knees, will you?" he said.

"There's nothing wrong with my knees!" I said indignantly. Cheek! He treats me like a child sometimes.

I pulled off my dirty clothes. My posh frock was hanging on the front of the wardrobe; Mrs Morris had washed and ironed it ready for today. It was a cotton effort in apple-green and white stripes. I put my white sandals on, too.

Then I heard the front door open, so I went downstairs. It was my sister Meg, with her arms full of Katey. She kissed my cheek.

"Charles is just struggling along with the goodies," she

said. Meg and Charles were bringing sausage rolls and things for the party.

"I'll leave the door open then," I said.

Fishpaste stopped licking himself and stretched his back into an arch. His mouth opened in a pink yawn. Katey gave a crow of delight and stretched her arms out to him. Meg handed my niece to me. She smelt deliciously of baby powder.

"You look nice," said Meg. She smiled at me.

At that moment, Charles came in. He filled the doorway with his enormous height and the kitchen seemed to shrink when he stepped in. He was laden with cake tins and plastic carrier bags.

"Hi, Lizzie – how's my favourite sister-in-law?" He kissed me soundly. "You look stunning – give us a twirl!"

"Let me take something before you drop it," said Meg.

They'd walked over from the next village, Penlorren, where they lived. It was only a ten minute walk along the coast road. They did have a car, but it was a waste of time driving over – there was nowhere to park in Penwithin – the streets were too narrow – so you had to leave your car parked at the top of the village, which is halfway back to Penlorren. They always walked when they came to see us.

I was just explaining about Rufus and the cake when there was another knock on the door. Meg opened it.

"Wendy!" she said. "Hello, come in!"

"I hope I'm not late," said a familiar voice. "Hello, everyone."

"Hello, Wendy," said the others, smiling.

"Hello, Miss Bullock," I said.

"Wendy," said Miss Bullock. "You must start calling me Wendy."

I didn't see why. Anyway, I couldn't – she was a

teacher, even if not *my* teacher, and I couldn't call a teacher by her Christian name, I simply *couldn't.* It didn't feel right.

We all beavered away, getting food out and putting it on to plates. We shooed Rufus and Fishpaste out into the back garden after Rufus snatched a sausage roll off the plate when our backs were turned. Mrs Morris and Ben arrived – Mrs Morris with a bag of chocolate éclairs and a bottle of whisky "for the birthday boy", Ben with several parcels wrapped in bright paper.

Finally, everything was ready. All the food was arranged on the scrubbed pine kitchen table, with the birthday cake in the pride of place in the middle. The bottle of whisky and a jug of lemonade stood, with the glasses, on the dresser. Charles had whipped something mysterious-looking from one of his carrier bags – it was bottle-shaped and foil-topped, and looked suspiciously like champagne – and put it in the fridge.

Through in the sitting room, all the presents were piled on a low table under the window and there was a crystal vase of red roses on the windowsill. It all looked lovely.

"Let's call Daddy," said Meg, looking eager. I yelled up the stairs: "Daddy, you can come down now!" I heard his footsteps come down the stairs. Then the kitchen door opened. Daddy stood there and looked slowly round at everything. His eyes stopped at my paper 'Happy Birthday' banner, and then looked at me. He smiled in a funny, sad sort of way.

"Sweetie," he said, and his voice sounded funny – as though he had a frog in his throat.

"Happy birthday, James," said Charles, his words breaking the odd silence which had descended on us.

"Happy birthday!" we all cried.

Charles started pouring out drinks - whisky for Daddy and himself, whisky and water for Meg, lemonade for the rest of us.

"Come and open your presents, Daddy!" I said and pulled him by the hand into the sitting room. We all piled in and watched him tearing into his birthday presents.

He was very lucky. He had all kinds of nice things - a shirt and sweater from Meg and Charles, aftershave from Ben, a silver pen and propelling pencil from Miss Bullock, and a slim little book which he opened and then quickly put aside.

I gave him a recording of Bach's double violin concerto and a box of cigars. He doesn't really smoke cigars, but I liked the box; it would make a nice container to keep things in, after the cigars were finished.

There was a big bar of chocolate from Rufus, and Fishpaste gave him a bunch of sweetpeas from the garden. I always have to buy the presents from Rufus and Fishpaste, and my pocket money doesn't stretch very far these days.

After he had exclaimed over them all, we let the animals in and went into the kitchen to eat the birthday tea. It was a lovely party. We all ate and drank until we were full; then I lit the candles on the birthday cake, and Daddy blew them all out and cut it. He made a little speech about reaching a great age and thanked me for reminding everyone by putting it on the cake and the banner. Charles thought that hugely funny and choked on a crumb. Meg had to thump him on the back. Mrs Morris muttered something about Charles going to meet his Maker sooner than expected.

"Good old Mrs M," whispered Daddy to Meg, "lugubrious as ever." I don't know what lugubrious means, but it sounded right somehow.

We all dived into the slices of birthday cake, and Rufus went around sniffing the floor and vacuuming up all the crumbs we'd dropped. The cake was quite good, which was a relief. Then Charles brought out his bottle from the fridge – it *was* champagne – and opened it with great ceremony.

"Charles - champagne!" said Daddy, pleased. It's his favourite. "How on earth can a vicar afford to buy champagne?" I forgot to say – Charles is the vicar of Penlorren, and he and Meg live in the huge vicarage there. The attics are great fun to explore. They're supposed to be haunted, but I haven't seen any ghosts there yet. Maybe one day.

We all drank some champagne – even Katey had some, off Meg's finger – and Daddy said something about how splendid it was to be with the people he loved at times like this.

I noticed that he was looking straight at Miss Bullock as he said it, and she was looking back at him with a funny little smile on her lips. I must admit, she did look rather nice. She was wearing a cotton dress in a beautiful shade of blue – Canaletto blue, I heard Daddy call it later – and her straight, square-cut fair hair was catching the sunlight through the window, so that it shone like spun silver. Daddy looked into her eyes, raised his glass and said, "To love!"

We all replied, "To love!" but, for some reason I didn't feel like drinking any more champagne. I put my glass down and wandered into the sitting room. I picked Fishpaste up and cuddled him. I felt rather peculiar inside.

Ben came in too. "What's up?" he asked.

"Up? Nothing. I'm OK," I replied, stroking my cat. Then everyone else came through into the room.

"I know what I'd really like – just to round the party off," said Daddy.

"What's that?" asked Meg, wiping Katey's chin.

"For Lizzie to play her violin."

So I did. I carefully tuned the strings; I rubbed rosin into the bow, I tucked the silk scarf into my neck, put my violin under my chin and began to play.

I played the Bach Chaconne – the famous one, from the second solo Partita. It seemed to suit my mood, the crashing chords bringing to my mind's eye the image of the Atlantic waves crashing against the Penwithin cliffs during a storm. It's quite tricky to play and lasts quite a long time – almost ten minutes – but everyone sat in silence. When I'd finished, there was a peculiar sort of pause. Then Mrs Morris said in hushed tones, "Twelve years old, and plays like the devil's got hold of her!"

"Mrs Morris!" Daddy doesn't like talk like that when Charles is around, although Charles doesn't mind a bit.

"Well, like an angel, then," Mrs Morris amended hastily. Everyone laughed.

I hope I don't seem a terrible show-off, playing in front of everybody like that. It's just what I do – and if I'm going to do it for my career, I've got to get used to audiences, haven't I?

When I finished the Bach, I put my violin away. Then we all gathered round the piano and sang. I accompanied – I'm not much good at proper piano music, Beethoven and Chopin and whatnot, but I do enjoy mucking around, making up accompaniments. We all sang things like 'Knees up Mother Brown' and 'By the Light of the Silvery Moon'. Then Charles sang a couple of things, accompanying himself. He's got a pretty good voice – he's used to singing all the 'Glory be to God on high' bits in church. But the things he sang now weren't a bit churchy. Daddy roared with laughter: Meg said he'd drunk too much champagne.

Then Miss Bullock sang. I must say, she has got a lovely voice. Apparently, she trained to be a singer before she decided to be a teacher. Anyway, she sang 'I know that my Redeemer liveth', from the *Messiah*. Luckily, we had an old score of the *Messiah* on top of the piano, so I could accompany her. We all applauded her when she'd finished and she gave a little curtsey. Daddy presented her with the bunch of sweetpeas Fishpaste had given him – I was a bit cross at that, but after all, they were his sweetpeas, to do what he wanted with.

After all that music, people started to go home. Daddy was out on the doorstep, saying goodnight to Miss Bullock, for ages. I went back into the sitting room and looked at all his presents. I saw the little book Miss Bullock had given him, half-hidden under the record. I pulled it out.

It was called *A Celebration of Love* and it had a picture of a man and woman gazing mistily into each other's eyes on the cover. I opened it. It was full of love poems – awfully slushy, most of them – and in the front was written 'To my darling Jamie, all my love always, WX.' I wondered who WX was. Then I realised that it was W – for Wendy – and a kiss: X.

I felt as though I'd been kicked in the tummy. I shoved the book back under the record and went back out into the kitchen. Daddy was still on the doorstep, saying goodnight to her.

I crept up the stairs and into my bedroom. Fishpaste was lying in his usual place in the middle of my bed. I got undressed, brushed my teeth and got into bed.

Fishpaste climbed on to my tummy and began to purr like a motorbike. He's not very sensitive to moods either. The trouble was, I didn't know what mood it was I was feeling. It felt suspiciously like jealousy. But I couldn't understand why I should be feeling jealous.

Daddy came up the stairs and poked his head around my door – at last, she'd gone home. Fishpaste miaowed at him. I pretended I was asleep.

But I wasn't, and I didn't get to sleep for ages.

3

Maudie

When I woke up the next morning, the sun was streaming through the window. My first thoughts were happy ones – what a lovely day, I'm glad to be alive. Then I remembered – school. Dimly, at the back of my mind, I remembered the events of yesterday evening and the book of poems. But I could only cope with one depressing thought at a time and, for the moment, the thought of school overshadowed everything else.

I was pretty mournful over my boiled egg. Daddy asked me what the matter was: "Too much champagne last night?" he said, with a grin. I bit into my toast.

"No," I replied shortly.

"I think you were up too late," Daddy said. "You must have been tired – you went to bed without saying goodnight."

"I know I did," I said. "You were such ages saying goodnight to Miss Thing, I'd have fallen asleep in the chair if I'd waited any longer." I didn't mention the poems.

Daddy looked puzzled. I felt a bit mean.

"What's wrong, sweetie?" he said gently.

"Oh, nothing – it's just the thought of school ..."

As I walked along the coast path (which was the way I always went to school – the same way as to Meg and Charles'), the thought of the day ahead didn't seem quite so bad after all. We wouldn't be doing much work – you never do, the first day of a new term, by the time you get your new timetable and everything – and I was going swimming with Ben later on the Strand.

In the playground I could see frightened-looking first-formers wandering around, looking lost. I knew exactly how they felt; the same as me, this time last year. It suddenly occurred to me that, now I was in the second form, I didn't feel lost and frightened any more. I knew my way around the school – huge, compared to my primary school – and knew some of the teachers. I was no longer a new girl. Feeling a little more cheerful, I hurried along to my new classroom.

When I got there, there was a bit of a commotion going on in the corner. The teacher hadn't arrived yet and there was a group of about four or five boys crowded around something I couldn't see. I went over to see what was going on.

Neil Trewin – typical, it's always him – and some of his cronies were chucking a pencil-case around. They were all jeering and shouting. I could see a figure standing in the middle of the crowd of boys, looking perplexed, not making any attempt to get the pencil-case back. It was a girl, pale and mousy-looking – the only colour about her was her flaming red hair, the colour beech-leaves go in the autumn. I decided she must be new. I watched the little ceremony with interest. Then, for some reason, I thought of Ben, alone and friendless at school, and I felt a pang of pity for the new girl.

"Neil Trewin – leave her alone! Don't be such a pig!" I said loudly. He looked at me curiously.

"What's the matter with you?" he said.

"Give her pencil-case back!" I demanded. A foxy look crossed his face.

"Lizzie Oliver loves Ben Polkerris!" he started to chant. His grotty friends joined in.

"Lizzie Oliver loves Ben Polkerris – Lizzie Oliver loves Ben ..." Much to my annoyance, I felt myself go red.

"Don't be so 'stupid," I said hotly. I said it hotly, because I felt hot.

But they soon got fed up. Neil put the pencil-case down after a bit and they wandered off, looking for someone else to annoy.

The new girl and I looked at each other. I must say, she looked a bit wet to me. Her face was pale and uninteresting – like the top of a semolina pudding. I noticed she had ginger freckles over her nose and her hair really was very bright, and frizzy: she reminded me a bit of Fishpaste on a bad day.

"What's your name?" I asked her, trying to be friendly. She said something I couldn't catch. At first, I thought she was speaking a foreign language; then I realised she just had a strong accent of some sort.

"What?" I said.

She said something that sounded like "Muddy". It couldn't be! Nobody's called Muddy! I had a brainwave.

"How d'you spell it?"

"M-A-U-D-I-E," she spelt.

"Oh – *Maudie!*" I said. It still seemed a pretty funny name to me. "Mine's Lizzie. Where do you come from?"

"Glasgy," she said.

"Where?" I'd never heard of it.

"Glasgy – Scortland." She was beginning to get the hang of it. "G-L-A-S-G-O-W."

"Oh – Glasgow!" I was starting to feel like a parrot.

Just then, the door opened and the form teacher, Mrs Britton, came in. She was very fat and everybody called her Great Britton: though not to her face, of course. She spotted Maudie and me in the corner.

"Ah – Lizzie and Maudie – you've made friends, I see. Good – you can sit next to each other then."

Maudie and I looked at each other. She looked quite pleased – I suppose she thought she could always spell everything to me. I didn't feel quite so happy about it – I'd rather have sat next to someone with whom conversation wasn't quite such hard work. Oh well – that's what you get for being friendly, I thought.

Great Britton handed out our new timetable forms, and we started copying the lessons from the blackboard. Then she called the register – I noticed that Maudie's surname was Campbell – and after that the bell went for Assembly. We all trooped into the school hall and stood in our straggly lines, waiting for the Headmaster (bow, grovel) to come in. For the rest of the day, Maudie and I were sat next to each other. I discovered that it was easier to understand what she was saying when she spoke whole sentences rather than single words.

She told me that her mother was an invalid, and had always wanted to come back to Cornwall when Maudie's father, who was Scottish, retired from his job in Glasgy – sorry, Glasgow. So here they were. Retired! – her father must be really old. I couldn't imagine Daddy retired: I'd be 32 when he did, pretty near retiring myself. I looked at Maudie with renewed interest. It must be strange to have such an old father.

On an impulse, I asked if she wanted to come home with me for tea. I knew Daddy wouldn't mind and Ben wasn't calling for me to go swimming until later. Maudie looked grateful and doubtful, both at the same time.

"I'll have tae phone me mother," she said (at least, that's what it sounded like).

When the bell finally went at the end of the day, Maudie and I walked to the school gate together. Some of my friends said goodbye as we passed them.

"See you tomorrow, Maudie," said Polly Adams, who's in my house. Maudie grasped my arm, her eyes shining.

"They said goodbye – they must like me! It's because you're sitting next to me!" I was embarrassed: I wasn't used to this sort of thing from my friends. I tried to take my arm away.

"Don't be daft – it's not because of me. They're friendly, that's all."

But she still held on to my arm as we crossed the playground.

"Does your mother have a wheelchair?" I asked, as we left the school behind us.

"Wheelchair? ... oh, no, she's not that sort of invalid. It's her lungs," Maudie said, looking sad. I still didn't understand, though.

When we got back to the cottage Daddy was out, so we ate tea on our own. The animals appeared as usual, ever-hopeful of food. I introduced them to Maudie, and she made a great fuss of Fishpaste.

"I had a wee kitten back home," she said, feeding Fishpaste with crab sandwich – greedy beast, they were far too good for him.

"What happened to it?" I asked, manoeuvring Fishpaste away with my foot.

"We had to get rid of him," Maudie explained. "Mummy couldn't breathe properly because of the fur." It seemed awfully bad luck for the kitten.

"Where's *your* mother?" asked Maudie suddenly.

There was a horrid pause; I couldn't think what to say. Luckily, Ben arrived just then to go swimming. I introduced him to Maudie as I cleared away the tea things. They didn't say anything to each other – they just looked. Then we left the cottage to walk Maudie home.

Ben and I had a gorgeous swim in the silken water around the next cove. Afterwards, we climbed up the cliff path and lay there on the top in the sun to dry off. It was still quite warm.

"Maudie says she can't swim," I remembered suddenly. "Don't you think she's a bit of a drip?"

"No, I don't," said Ben. "I thought she was rather nice. Pretty."

I sat up in amazement.

"Pretty? Are you barmy?"

"*I* thought she was pretty," said Ben again. His eyes were closed. "Like a dormouse – or a squirrel."

"Huh!" He had a funny idea of prettiness – a dormouse, indeed! I lay down again. For some reason, I felt cross. "Do you think *I'm* pretty?" I asked him.

He opened one eye and looked at me lazily.

"No," he said. He closed it again.

I felt even crosser. I was also beginning to get chilly, so I started to pull my clothes on over my swimsuit. Then, out of the blue, I remembered the book Miss Bullock had given Daddy.

"Ben," I said slowly. "If a lady gives a man a book with slushy poems in it – and if she writes 'with all my love' in it – do you suppose that means they're in love?"

Ben considered.

"I should think so," he said. "Probably."

A cloud passed over the sun. I shivered.

"Come on," I said. "Let's go home."

4

Ben writes a Letter

I was quite pleased to find that school that term wasn't half as bad as I thought it was going to be. For some reason, Maudie and I became quite friendly: I say 'for some reason' because she wasn't really the sort of person I was usually friendly with. She *was* drippy – I don't care what Ben said – and she would follow me around like some overgrown dog, pathetically grateful to me for noticing her. To tell you the truth, she irritated me. Daddy said she was like a long drink of water, which I think is a very good description.

But when she was teased, which was often in those first few weeks of term, I would always find myself leaping to defend her. I got cross with myself for doing it, because the more I did it, the more pathetic she would become. I thought she ought to try and stand up for herself more. But I couldn't help it – it was a sort of reflex. I kept thinking of Ben away at school with no special friend to stick up for him, and I told myself I was doing it for *him*. Charles, being a vicar, says that we all have a cross to bear. I suppose Maudie was my cross, sort of.

The days went by, and autumn was upon us. It was a beautiful autumn, as though the summer didn't want to end, although you could feel the winter approaching by the nip in the air in the evenings. Ben had gone back to school and I missed him badly. Maudie wasn't the same. I couldn't confide in her as I could with Ben: she didn't understand how important it was to me that I had a career in music. She wanted to get married and have babies when she grew up. Well, I suppose I do too – at some stage. But not at once.

I also couldn't talk to Maudie about Miss Bullock, although I had finally told her about my mother, and the Awful Time. To my surprise, she was very kind about it. I was a bit upset, and she lent me her hanky and looked the other way until I'd finished being upset.

Miss Bullock was at the cottage one day when Maudie came for tea. They chattered away for ages – about school mostly. I felt quite left out. Afterwards, when I was walking Maudie home, she started saying how nice Miss Bullock was. She went on and on.

"Is your father going to marry her?" she asked. I remembered the book of poems and shivered.

"Don't be stupid!" I said scathingly. "Why on earth should he marry her?" The thought horrified me.

"They seem awful fond of each other," Maudie went on.

"She just helps out," I said, not quite truthfully, I'm afraid. I didn't want to think about it.

Maudie played the recorder. When she told me I was ever so pleased because I don't often get the chance to play with people my own age. But she wasn't very good. I usually accompanied her on the piano – it was good practice for me, although not as much fun as 'Knees up Mother Brown' – but she usually stopped every time she made a mistake, to apologize. As she made tons of mistakes, we did a lot of stopping and not much playing. But it was OK. It was a bit like having a little sister to boss around, which I'd never had, although Maudie was already thirteen – six months older than me.

Charles persuaded Maudie and me to sing in the choir at his church. The choirmaster was a tall, thin man with incredibly long fingers – his name was Mr Trotter. He wore one of those black teachers' gowns and he had a long thin body to match his fingers. When he conducted us he would crouch over the music stand, and in his flapping black gown he looked for all the world like a crow about to take off.

For the services, he would put his University hood on, to show he had learnt music properly. It wasn't *really* a hood; he didn't wear it over his head: it went round his shoulders like a fur shawl and hung down his back in a long, pointed, furry V. I coveted that hood – some day, I promised myself, I'll have one of those.

Maudie was madly in love with Mr Trotter. Whenever he addressed all the trebles she would go bright red. She wrote long love-letters to him, which she never sent. She always tore them up with a sigh. One day at practice he actually spoke directly to her.

"Maudie," he said, "will you hand the hymn books round, please?"

She blushed scarlet and dropped *Hymns Ancient and Modern Revised* all over the floor. Then she missed all the trebles' entries during the practice. Honestly. I can't see the attraction myself.

Because Maudie was in love with Mr Trotter, she never missed a practice; which was a bit of a drag, because that meant I had to go to them all as well. I wouldn't have minded missing one occasionally, but

Daddy said I had to be committed about it. It was all right for *him* to say that – he didn't have to do violin practice and piano practice. *And* all my homework. I was very busy.

But if I didn't go to the rehearsals with Maudie, she wouldn't have been allowed to, either. As it was, Mrs Campbell was dead reluctant to let her, until she found out the vicar was my brother-in-law. But I did privately wonder what Mrs Campbell would have thought about Maudie's real reason for wanting to sing in the church choir.

Eventually, half-term came and Ben was home for a week. The first time I saw him over the holidays was in church on the Sunday morning. He was standing in the pew with his family, between Ruth and Rebecca, his sisters. I waved to him during the first hymn. Maudie looked to see who I was waving to, and went red when she saw Ben. Mr Trotter frowned at us both and she went even redder. It clashed horribly with her hair!

Afterwards, Daddy and I were invited to lunch with the Polkerrises, and afterwards Ben and I went for our favourite walk over the cliffs. It was much colder now it was late October, although the sun was still shining bravely. The sea was very blue below us, the seagulls searching for food in earnest now that winter was nearly here.

I told Ben about Maudie and Mr Trotter. He seemed to want to talk about Maudie a lot and asked if we both wanted to go for a bike ride with him the next day.

" I doubt her mother will let her," I said.

"Why not?" asked Ben, surprised.

"She never wants her to do anything," I told him. I was unused to having to ask permission to do everything, but Maudie always had to. The answer was frequently 'no', too.

"Poor Maudie," mused Ben.

I didn't think she was poor; I thought she was wet. But something made me hold back from saying this.

"Why don't we go on our own?" I suggested. "We could ride to Tintagel and have a picnic."

Ben thought this a great idea, so we arranged to meet early the next morning. I nearly rang Maudie when Daddy and I got home that afternoon, to ask her to join us on our trip to Tintagel. But I didn't. I convinced myself that she wouldn't have been allowed to, anyway.

Ben and I had a good day – Tintagel is reckoned to be the ruins of King Arthur's Camelot – and it was past six o'clock when we got back to Penwithin, exhausted. Daddy told me Maudie had rung while I was out. By the time I'd had a hot bath and eaten my supper, I couldn't be bothered to ring her back. I really couldn't face her going on and on about Mr Trotter as usual.

I didn't see anything of Maudie for the rest of half-term either – there seemed to be so much else to do – and I wasn't that surprised not to see her back at school when it started again. To be honest, I didn't think much about it – seeing Ben again had pushed Maudie into the background – but I decided she probably had a cold. She was dead unhealthy, always seemed to have the sniffles; at least, that's what I told myself. Ordinarily I'd have gone round to see her – of course I would! – but somehow, with Ben being home and everything, I never got round to it. If I'd have known then what I later found out, I'd have gone to see her immediately. It was to play on my conscience later.

Ben went back to school a few days after me (his holidays are always longer, lucky pig!). The day before he was due back I had this really weird phone call from him when I got home from school.

"Er," he said.

"Is that you, Ben?" I demanded.

"Are you alone?" he asked.

"What do you mean?" I said. "Rufus and Fishpaste are here, but I don't suppose they're bothered about anything you want to say."

"Ha jolly ha," Ben said acidly. He changed tack slightly. "Are you doing anything?"

"Yes," I said crossly. I was getting fed up with this. "I'm speaking to you on the phone. Are you going to tell me what you want or not? Cos if you're not ..."

"OK, OK," he muttered. "Sorry. It's just ... look, can you meet me on the cliffs, say, in ten minutes?"

I was intrigued. "Yes, I s'pose so. Why?"

"Just come. Oh, and Lizzie – come alone," he said darkly and rang off.

I had a terrible job trying to keep Rufus inside the cottage – he always thinks me going out means 'walkies' – but I bribed him with dog chocs and rushed out, and up on to the cliffs. Ben was already there. He must have really belted up here, I thought – his face was all red.

"Hi," I said, out of breath. "What's up? What's all the mystery about?"

"Oh, nothing." He was very offhand. "Look – did you see Maudie today?"

"No – I told you, she's off school. Got a cold or something."

"Oh." He sounded disappointed. "Well, when you see her," he rummaged in his jeans pocket, "can you give her this?" He held out a white envelope, crumpled and dirty, with 'Maudie' written on the front in fountain-pen ink.

"What is it?" I asked.

"What does it look like, stupid? It's a letter, of course.

You will give it to her, won't you?"

"Is that it? Is that what you've been all secretive about?" A sudden thought occurred to me. "Hey, it's not a love-letter, is it?" I asked suspiciously.

"No! It's just a letter, that's all. You're not to open it, though," he said accusingly.

"Cheek! I don't read other people's letters!" But I was curious. "Are you *sure* it's not a love-letter?" I held it up to the light.

Ben went red. "Shut up, Lizzie! I've told you, it's just a letter – now, will you give it to her or not?"

I considered it. "Depends," I said, sniffing.

"On what?" Ben demanded.

"On whether you say please, you pig. After all, I am doing you a favour." I felt cross at Ben's assumption that I would just do as he wanted.

A more relaxed look came across his face. "Sorry, Lizzie. Please, please, O dear friend, please do as I bid thee, and I will be thy friend for life."

I grinned. "OK then, seeing as it's you. Looking forward to going back to school, are we, Polkerris?"

Ben punched me lightly on the arm. "Oh, shut up, Oliver ..."

We went back down the cliff path together, teasing each other, friends again.

5

Getting ready for Christmas

Maudie was at school the next day. I was quite
pleased to see her and told her all about what Ben
and I had done over half-term.

"It all sounds lovely," she said wistfully.

I asked her why she hadn't been at school last week.
Apparently, she'd caught a cold at the beginning of half-
term, which her mother then picked up. But because Mrs
Campbell's lungs were weak (due to her illness) the cold
had infected them, and on the Monday evening she was
rushed into hospital because she couldn't breathe.

"Is she all right now?" I asked anxiously.

"She's better than she was. She's coming home next
week, but she'll have to stay in bed a wee while."

"You should have rung me," I said guiltily. "I'd have
come round to see you."

"I did," replied Maudie. "I rang on Monday, but you
were out, your Dad said. I didn't want to bother you
again ..." she trailed off.

I felt ashamed of myself. Poor Maudie: unwell, and
worried about her mother, while I was off gallivanting,
as Mrs Morris said, around the countryside with Ben. I
really felt awful.

That episode changed our whole friendship, I think – Maudie's and mine, I mean. I can't really explain what happened, but we became much closer: more sort of equal. I stopped thinking of her as a kind of dimmer little sister and started treating her as a friend. When she was teased now at school, I would bite my tongue until she defended herself. *Then* I would stick up for her; not before. She still irritated me at times though – I suppose she always would. It was just part of our friendship. She would call me bossy at times. I suppose she was right, although I don't like to admit it, because that's what Mrs Morris used to call me: Little Miss Bossy Boots. Maudie didn't call me Little Miss, though: that *would* have been pushing her luck.

Oh yes – and I gave her Ben's letter. I found it, screwed up and dirty, in my coat pocket about two weeks later. I'd totally forgotten about it, but Maudie didn't seem to mind. She let me read it – it seemed a pretty ordinary letter for Ben to have made such a fuss about, that's all I can say.

It just said, "*Dear Maudie, I hope you are well, I am very well,*" and then it went on to tell her about all his lessons, and what his school's football and rugby scores had been so far that term. Ben wrote remarkably uninteresting letters – it was dead boring, really. I'm sure Maudie wasn't interested in the football and rugby scores. I know I wasn't. But Maudie said it was sweet of him to have written, and she wrote back.

I think they carried on writing to each other, but I'm not sure. I wasn't really bothered, one way or the other.

The days went by, and autumn slid gently into winter. When you live in the country or by the sea, you're very aware of the seasons changing. Not like living in a city –

I couldn't bear it, I thought, not seeing the leaves on the trees turning colour and finally dropping off; not seeing the new buds forming every spring, and finally the miracle of new, fresh green leaves bursting into life. How awful to miss all that! If I'd known what Fate had in store for me I wouldn't have been so smug.

I was beginning to look forward to Christmas, although it had very mixed associations for me – ever since that awful Christmas two years ago, when we all sat around feeling numb. We'd realised on the 28th that we hadn't opened any presents, but it seemed wrong to then. It was a horrible Christmas.

I hadn't been looking forward to it as much as usual, anyway, because someone at school the previous year had told me the truth about Santa Claus. I'd had my suspicions, anyway, but it's still a bit of a shock when you find out it's really been your parents all along. But that was nothing compared to the shock of suddenly only having one parent.

The following Christmas – last year – hadn't been too bad, although we were all making a really huge effort to enjoy ourselves. But this year: this year felt different. I could already feel the old familiar excitement creeping up on me. We were all going to Meg and Charles' for Christmas dinner – everyone, including Ben and his family, and Miss Bullock. And Katey was there this year: her first ever Christmas. And we could always hope for snow, although we hadn't had a properly white Christmas for ages.

Meg drove Maudie and me to Truro the Saturday before Christmas, to buy presents. Truro was full of eager, busy shoppers. It was bitterly cold – it felt like snow – and we were all wrapped up in hats and scarves. The tip of Maudie's nose had turned red and she looked more like a squirrel than ever. Meg had on her soft, fluffy grey coat and she looked like a cuddly teddy bear.

We bought loads of presents. I spent all the pocket money I'd saved up and I had to borrow from Meg to buy Daddy's present. Meg bought loads of new decorations for the Christmas tree. Maudie hung around the menswear departments in the shops, imagining what sweater she'd buy for Mr Trotter if *she* were married to him, instead of his wife. I think she secretly enjoyed all this mooning about. It got on my nerves rather, but I had to try to sympathize, because she was my friend.

Meg bought us hot chocolate and sticky cakes in a teashop near the Cathedral. Then we went to Evensong – Afternoon-song, really, because it was only four o'clock. It was nice to hear the singing done properly for a change. Although we all enjoyed singing in Charles' church choir, nobody could pretend we were very good. Mrs Rogers, who was a contralto, had a voice which swooped around, and wobbled alarmingly on high notes. Mr Porter was supposed to be a bass, but all the notes he sang sounded the same. I think he was tone-deaf. I'm glad I didn't stand next to him: it was dreadfully offputting.

The Cathedral choir didn't do anything like that. It was all beautifully sung, like the radio.

Before we knew where we were, it was Christmas Eve. Daddy and I drove to where Mummy is buried to put flowers on her grave. I looked at the headstone; all the writing became blurred and my throat felt tight. I looked away.

"Why don't you go and make sure Rufus is all right, sweetie?" said Daddy. We'd left Rufus in the car, otherwise he'd have gone bounding all over the cemetery, which wouldn't have been very appropriate. Rufus didn't understand these things.

I let him out of the back of the car and clipped his lead on. We went for a run in a field opposite the cemetery; then I put him back in the car. It was getting dark. We ought to be getting back home: Ben was coming for tea. I went back into the cemetery to get Daddy.

He was kneeling at the foot of Mummy's grave, on the cold damp grass.

"Anna," he said. "Anna." Just like that – very softly and sadly. Anna was my mother's name. Then he said something very odd.

"Forgive me," he said. "She needs a mother."

I felt peculiar, watching Daddy kneeling there – as though I was spying on him. I coughed, to let him know I was there. He stood up, and brushed down the knees of his trousers. Then he walked over to me and, holding my hands, he crouched down so that he had to look up at me.

He looked into my eyes. His were wet, as though the wind had got to them. But there was no wind.

"Lizzie," he said seriously, "I love you. Whatever happens, remember that."

I nodded. I knew he loved me – he didn't have to say so. But it seemed important to him to tell me.

Then he stood up – knees cracking – and he pulled me to him. We stood there in the cemetery with our arms tight round each other. I buried my face in his jacket, smelling his familiar Daddy smell. For a fleeting moment I felt achingly sad. Then we walked off together in the fading grey winter light, to go home for our tea.

6

Christmas at the Vicarage

On Christmas Eve, when Ben had gone home after tea, Daddy and I loaded the car down with all the things we were taking to Meg's, including the animals. It looked as though we were going away for a month, not just a night. Then we drove over to the vicarage.

It was lovely and warm inside: the weather outside was really freezing. It *did* feel as though it might snow. After saying hello to Meg and Charles, I wandered into the vast sitting room with Fishpaste following close behind. He'd been to the vicarage before, tons of times. He leapt on to the piano stool and began to clean himself.

The room looked stunning. There was a huge Christmas tree in the corner by the stone fireplace – it must have been easily three metres tall (the tree I mean, not the fireplace). It was trimmed with the decorations Meg had bought in Truro, and already there were stacks of exciting-looking parcels scattered beneath it. I squeezed one or two, to see if I could guess what was in them. I recognised the feel of a pair of slippers in one for Charles. What boring presents grown-ups get! I hoped I wasn't getting any slippers. The tree also had tiny, lighted candles all over it – when I looked closer I could see that they were actually electric ones, but they looked very realistic. There was a gleaming golden star on top. It did look beautiful.

The rest of the room was decorated with masses of Christmas cards, strung down the walls on red ribbon streamers. Each streamer had a bunch of holly and mistletoe fixed to the top, and there were huge wreaths of holly, mistletoe and ivy and red ribbon attached to the wall and on top of all the pictures. The piano had a silver candelabra on its top, with red candles like twisted sticks of barley-sugar in it. There were old-fashioned brass candle-lamps dotted about the room. It all looked so Christmassy and special: I was beginning to feel really excited.

Just then, the door pushed open and Rufus came wagging in, grinning broadly. He'd been investigating the kitchen, where they were making mulled wine by the smell of it. Someone had put some red tinsel around his collar: he looked very smart and pleased with himself. Together, we went to look over the presents.

Later that evening, some neighbours came round. It seemed funny to hear them call Charles 'Father'. I know it sounds stupid, but I always forget he's a vicar, despite them living in a vicarage and me seeing him in church and everything. I suppose it's because you always expect vicars to be serious, pious sorts of people. But Charles isn't a bit like that – not at all preachy. My sister wouldn't have married him if he had been, anyway.

We had mulled wine and savoury bits – canopies, I think they're called – and mincepies and glorious, sticky marzipan *petits fours*. Rufus had a wonderful time sucking up to everybody, getting them to give him bits. Anybody would think we never fed him - he always lets us down like that. Fishpaste sat on a pile of music in the corner, looking cross. He's not a terribly sociable cat – not when there's lots of people around anyway – and he was jealous of all the attention Rufus was getting. I gave him two biscuits with sardine pâté on - that cheered him up a bit.

After everybody had gone we cleared up all the glasses and Meg had to put the vacuum cleaner round to pick up all the bits of pastry people had trodden into the carpet. It would have been much quicker just to let Rufus go round. Then it was time to go to Midnight Mass. I love Midnight Mass: I suppose that's when Christmas *really and truly* begins for me. This year was the first I'd sung in the choir. The service was lovely. It started off with us - the choir - processing through the darkened church, carrying candles, singing "Once in Royal David's City". Mr Trotter walked in front of us, waving his long fingers around over his head so that we could see what he was conducting. I felt sorry for Mr Osborne, who plays the organ: he had to play in the dark, by feel, because if he'd turned his little light on, it would have spoiled the effect. Anyway, we wandered up the aisle in the dark, trying not to trip over our robes. We had quite a job concentrating on that, whilst holding all our music in one hand and a lighted candle in the other, but it must have looked lovely from the congregation. I tripped going up the chancel steps, and hot wax dripped on to my hand, and I nearly shrieked – I just stopped myself in time.

The church looked beautiful - as it must have done in the olden days, before electricity, when it was first built. And I could see my breath puff into the darkness as I sang. It was magical. Charles very cleverly timed his sermon to finish just on midnight: he ended by saying "and a merry Christmas to you all!" and, as we looked at our watches, we saw that it was indeed Christmas Day.

Afterwards, in the choir vestry, I said 'Merry Christmas' to the rest of the choir and gave them all their cards. I was sorry that Maudie wasn't there – she'd gone to Scotland with her parents for Christmas. I was rather a long time saying goodnight to the choir and, when I finally came out, everybody was waiting in the porch for me. Charles and Daddy were grinning happily.

"There she is!" said Meg. Katey, wrapped in a white woollen bonnet and mittens, gurgled.

"Look, Lizzie, look!" said Meg.

"Come here, Lizzie – look!" said Daddy. He put his arm around my shoulders and pointed out into the night. "Look!"

I looked out into the dark Christmas morning. All around, huge white flakes were falling. It was snowing.

I awoke next morning to a mysterious silent white glow over everything. Fishpaste was still asleep on the duvet, but when I looked at my watch it was half past nine! I'd overslept on Christmas Day – unheard of! The others must have gone to the morning service without me, I thought. Then I saw a large, lumpy stocking at the foot of my bed and all other thoughts flew away ...

When I'd opened all the presents in the stocking and eaten half the bar of chocolate and the tangerine, I let Rufus into the bedroom and gave him the rest of the chocolate. Then I got up and had a wash, and put on the new Christmas dress Daddy had given me. It was shiny royal blue taffeta. Very posh. By the time I'd done all that, I could hear the others coming back from church, so I went downstairs.

The kitchen was filled with glorious smells: the turkey roasting, the mincepies, fresh percolating coffee, the brandy Charles was pouring. Everybody was happy and chattering excitedly. We all said 'Merry Christmas' to each other, and I ate my breakfast and the others had coffee with brandy in it – to keep the cold out, Meg said. It was lovely and warm in the kitchen, but Charles had had to clear a path to the church with a shovel that morning. He said, "It's a foot deep in places. I hope Wendy and the Polkerrises manage to get over."

I knew they would. It was a gorgeous winter's day, the sun shining from a perfect blue sky, making the snow sparkle. When I let Rufus out, he ploughed around excitedly in the snow and barked at it. Fishpaste wasn't so keen – he walked slowly in Rufus' pawmarks, like King Wenceslas' page, and shook each paw fastidiously. I didn't really blame him: I wouldn't have wanted to go out with no shoes on, either.

After breakfast, we all went into the sitting room. Charles put a record of Christmas carols on, and we all got down to the serious business of opening our presents.

I can't say what we all had: it would take too long. But we all had lots of lovely things, including the animals. They got various tins of food – Fishpaste had a whole tin of tuna fish (his favourite), all to himself. They both had smart new collars and Rufus had a new lead. He also had a box of choc-drops and Fishpaste a catnip mouse, which he was promptly sick on. It must have been all the excitement. They played with all the wrapping paper, then lay down suddenly and went to sleep.

After that, Ben and his family arrived, wrapped up in

coats and scarves and wearing wellingtons. While they were taking off their layers of outer clothing, the doorbell went again and there stood Miss Bullock. It took ages for them all to stamp the snow from their boots and get their coats and things off.

"Come through into the warm," Charles said, "and have a drink. That'll warm you up!"

Meg got confused and gave Ben a glass of sherry, which he drank anyway.

"I quite like it," he said.

Charles and Ben's Dad whistled when Miss Bullock finally came in: Daddy just stared. She was wearing a wine-coloured velvet dress with white lace at the throat and wrists. She looked like Alice in Wonderland, in white lacey tights and low-heeled shoes the same colour as the dress. No wonder they whistled. Ben was staring, too – most unlike him.

At last it was time for lunch, and what a lunch it was! There were ten of us around the dining table – eleven, if you count Katey – and it was festooned with evergreens and laden with candles and crackers.

And food! The turkey, roast potatoes, boiled potatoes, brussels sprouts, carrots, parsnips; three types of stuffing. Little sausages wrapped in bacon. Cranberry sauce, bread sauce, steaming fragrant gravy.

When we had finished that lot, we had Christmas pudding and brandy butter. Then mincepies and cream, and coffee. The grown-ups had liqueurs with their coffee. We all pulled our crackers and read the jokes and put on the paper hats. There was a lot of noise and laughter. Daddy proposed a toast: "To the Cook!" We all drank: "To Meg!" Then Charles gave her a sideways look, and said "Why don't we tell them now?"

She glanced at Charles uncertainly: he took her hand

and nodded at her, smiling.

"Go on lovey: tell them!" he encouraged.

"Well – Charles and I – well, me actually; I'm going to have another baby."

I felt really pleased.

"A baby sister for Katey!" I cried.

"Or a brother," said Meg, smiling.

"Well well well; when's the happy event?" asked Daddy. He looked thrilled.

"Some time in August: the middle, we think," answered Charles, squeezing Meg's hand.

"How super for you both," said Miss Bullock. She and Daddy exchanged what are known as meaningful glances, but at the time I didn't realise just how meaningful ...

Finally, when we could eat and drink no more, we left the table. We cleared the table and stacked the dishes in the dishwasher. Ben and I went for a walk in the snow with Ruth and Rebecca. I had to borrow a pair of Meg's wellingtons, as I hadn't brought any with me, and put on four pairs of socks to make them fit. We took Rufus with us and went down into Penlorren as far as the Post Office. We hardly saw a soul – everybody must have been inside, watching TV. We could see our footsteps in the snow, stretching back up the hill. We threw snowballs at each other and Rufus went bonkers with excitement, barking and leaping around. We threw snowballs at him, too. He loved it: he tried to eat the snow. It was great.

Then we went back to the vicarage. Ruth and Becky built a snowman in the back garden, which slopes and is vast. I went inside and borrowed one of Meg's tea-trays. We used it as a sledge and went up and down the sloping garden until it eventually grew too dark to see. So we went indoors, leaving the snowman to watch silently over the garden.

Meg had made tea, but nobody had much of an appetite after the huge lunch. She'd made a cake and iced it in white peaks, so that it looked like a snow scene. She'd stuck a miniature reindeer, Santa Claus and fir tree on it. It looked nice. I decided I could just about manage a small piece, so I did. Then I discovered I *was* hungry after all. It must have been all that sledging on the tea-tray. After tea, we played charades, only it was better than usual because we dressed up. Ben put one of Charles' dog-collars on and did *The Book of Genesis* (you know, from the Bible), but nobody guessed it.

Then someone – Daddy, I think – suggested we play

Sardines. The vicarage is the most perfect house to play Sardines in – it's got loads of hidden nooks and crannies.

When it was my turn to go off and hide, I went up into the attics. You get up there through a door in Meg and Charles' bedroom – it looks just like a cupboard door until you open it and see the stairs going up. It was cold and dark and rather spooky: I seemed to be up there, alone, for ages and was beginning to get a bit scared. Then, at last, the door opened and I could see a figure coming towards me.

"Lizzie?" it whispered. It was Miss Bullock. "Are you the Sardine?" She obviously didn't know how to play the game. I thought I'd better help her out.

"Yes," I whispered back.

Then she did an odd thing. She kissed my cheek. I could smell her face-powder, and the scent she used. Memories of Mummy flooded over me and I had a lump in my throat.

"Merry Christmas, Lizzie," she whispered. "I hope we're going to be really good friends."

I wonder why she said that? I thought. She's Daddy's friend, not mine. Still, I do rather like her. Then we stood there together, in the dark, and waited for the others to come and find us.

I look back on that day as the last of the happy times – it was shortly afterwards that everything started to change. And for the worse. Positively, definitely for the worse.

7

I get a Shock

The rest of the Christmas holidays passed by really quickly – as holidays always do, and soon it was New Year's Eve. I was looking forward to the New Year – I could start keeping the diary Ben had given me for Christmas. Daddy was taking Miss Bullock to a dinner-dance in a nearby town and Mrs Morris was coming over that evening, to sit with me. I was cross: I knew Daddy meant baby sit. I do hate the way adults treat you like kids, even if you're really quite grown-up. I was to be thirteen in March – quite old enough to be on my own for an evening.

Anyway, Daddy insisted. Meg and Charles and Katey were going to see some friends, so they couldn't come over, and Daddy said nobody should be on their own on New Year's Eve. I was allowed to stay up late – there was a good film on TV – so I didn't mind too much. It was just the principle of having a baby-sitter.

Miss Bullock came over that afternoon so she could get changed at the cottage – she was using my bedroom. She was also staying overnight: Daddy was going to sleep on the sofa-bed in his study and she was sleeping

in Daddy's bed. It was all a bit like the Three Bears:
"Who's been sleeping in *my* bed?"

When Daddy came downstairs, he looked stunning.
Terribly smart. He was wearing his dinner-jacket, which
he said he rarely got the chance to wear these days. He
had a black bow-tie on, too – a proper one which you
tied, not one on elastic which Daddy rather scorned. I
don't know why; he could never tie the real thing
properly. I had to neaten it up for him.

Then the sitting room door opened and Miss Bullock
came in. Daddy's jaw nearly hit the ground and I stared
at her. I couldn't help it. She was wearing a dress of
palest dove-grey. The front was very daring, and then it
fell to the ground in soft silken folds. She had diamonds
around her throat and in her ears, and her pale blonde
hair was swept up on top of her head in an unfamiliar
style. Her scent filled the room – it was gorgeous, like a
meadow full of flowers or the smell of fresh clean linen.

"Will I do?" she asked in a small voice. Daddy
chuckled.

"Do? – I should say so! You'll knock 'em all out!" he
said.

"You look lovely," I told her. "Like a model."

"Thank you, Lizzie," she said solemnly. "Shall I give
you a twirl?" She turned on her heel and wafts of
perfume tantalised my nostrils.

"We must be off, Jamie," she said to Daddy. He put his
wellingtons and overcoat on.

"I'll just fetch the car," he said to Miss Bullock. "I
shan't be long. You stay here in the warm." He kissed
me. "'Night, sweetie: Happy New Year. Don't you wait up
for us – we'll be late." Then he was gone, through the
front door, in an icy blast.

When Daddy sounded his horn I went to the door

with Miss Bullock. On a sudden impulse, I reached up and kissed her cheek.

"Have a lovely time," I said. She looked at me in surprise.

"Why, Lizzie – thank you. Happy New Year."

Then she went. I was later to regret that kiss.

Mrs Morris arrived as they were driving up the hill. She came in, mournful as ever, stamping her feet and complaining about the weather. A thaw had just begun to set in and the snow outside was turning into a horrid slushy mess.

We had some supper together in front of the TV. I toasted crumpets before the fire and we spread them with butter and potted meat. You-know-who appeared as if by magic – the two you-know-whos, I should say. We gave them some to shut them up.

I changed into my night things so I could go to bed as soon as the film ended. Mrs Morris and I watched TV in companionable silence, eating chocolates. Mrs Morris had brought her knitting – she was knitting a little coat for Meg's new baby. I had Fishpaste on my lap – the coat looked just the right size for him. He'd have looked sweet in it, I thought.

I must have fallen asleep. The next thing I knew, I was lying, squashed up, on the sofa: the television was off and the fire was burning low, its embers glowing redly in the darkness of the room. Somebody had put a blanket over me.

I stretched, and stood up. I could hear low voices in the kitchen and went to investigate. The old clock on the mantelpiece said ten past one: the New Year had arrived.

I got as far as the kitchen door and stood still in surprise. For Daddy and Miss Bullock were standing there in their finery, their arms tightly around each other. Daddy was kissing her. The kiss seemed to go on for ages. I felt embarrassed, but was rooted to the spot. I couldn't move.

Finally, the kiss ended.

"I'll make you happy, Wendy," Daddy said to her in a thick voice. "I swear I won't disappoint you."

Then they noticed me.

They moved slowly apart, as though they were under water. They didn't seem at all bothered that I'd caught them at it. Daddy had a soppy look on his face. I think he'd been drinking. He took me by the hand and led me into the kitchen. I sat down on a stool. I still felt half asleep.

"Lizzie," said Daddy, "we have something very exciting to tell you." He reached for Miss Bullock's hand. They stood there, smiling down at me like a couple of stupid sheep. "This evening," he went on, "Wendy did me the honour of accepting my proposal of marriage. She is going to become my wife."

At first, I couldn't understand why Daddy was talking in that funny, formal way. Then it hit me what he'd said.

Marriage. He was going to *marry* her. I felt as though someone had taken the stool away from under me. I couldn't say anything: I just sat there and stared at them, aghast.

"Aren't you going to congratulate us?" asked Daddy, beaming at her. "Aren't you pleased? After all, Wendy's going to be your mother – well, your stepmother, at any ..."

I couldn't bear to hear any more. I put my hands over my ears and stood up, knocking the stool over in my haste.

"Shut up!" I shouted. "Shut up! She's *not* going to be

my mother – she can't be, nobody can! My mother's dead – *dead*!" I ran from the room, locked myself in my bedroom, and threw myself on my bed. Great sobs wracked my body – I couldn't seem to get my breath. I couldn't believe it: Daddy, marrying *her*? I thought of how I'd kissed her cheek that evening, and shuddered. How could he marry her – how *could* he? I thought. There was a tap on the door. It was Daddy.

"Lizzie?" he said. "Lizzie, can I come in? Lizzie, don't be like this – let me in!"

I didn't answer. He kept trying to talk to me through the door. Eventually, I heard *her* voice outside.

"Leave her be, Jamie," she murmured. "Things might look different in the morning."

I hated the way she called my father Jamie. Why couldn't she call him James, like everybody else did?

They went away at last. I heard them go downstairs. I quietly opened the door and let my cat in – he was sitting on the landing, as I knew he would be, puzzled as to why I'd shut him out. He jumped on to the bed, purring. I buried my face in his ginger fur and cried saltily into his side. I couldn't bear it. Why did Daddy have to get married again – *why*? I didn't understand it at all. And I'd do anything I could to stop it happening.

8

An awful New Year

When I woke up the next morning, I saw my brand-new diary on my bedside table. All the previous night's happenings came flooding back in a horrid rush, and I grabbed a pen and scribbled furiously in the diary, to make me feel better.

1st January.

Dear Diary,
What a rotten, beastly start to the New Year! Daddy says he's going to marry Miss Bullock – why does she have to go and spoil things? We were perfectly happy the way we were, just Daddy and me. I hate her. She's a horrible old bag. I bet she's only after a new surname; if I was called Bullock I'd want to change it too. But I don't want her as an Oliver. I hate her.

I felt a twinge of guilt when I read this back – after all, she could hardly help her surname, could she? And I wasn't sure that I actually hated her as such. I still couldn't see why Daddy wanted to marry her, though – why, she was years and years younger than him.

We were supposed to be going to Meg's for lunch – I really didn't feel like it. I guessed they were going to tell

Meg and Charles the news today – I wonder how *they* will react, I thought. I supposed she would be Meg's stepmother, too: and Charles' stepmother-in-law – how odd! Katey will have a stepgrandmother who's younger than her father. The thought didn't amuse me at all. It was ridiculous. How could Daddy do it, without thinking about all this?

I was sitting on the edge of my bed when there was a tap at the door. It opened before I had a chance to say anything: I'd unlocked it earlier, to let Fishpaste downstairs. It was Daddy.

"Can I come in, Lizzie?" he said. It seemed an unnecessary question, as he was already in.

"I suppose so," I mumbled, not looking at him.

"Oh, sweetie," he said solemnly, sitting down beside me on the bed. "What a start to a New Year! Let's not quarrel."

"Well, it's *your* fault!" I cried. "How *can* you marry her, Daddy? She's far too young for you!"

Daddy laughed. He actually *laughed* – I was furious, I can tell you.

"Oh, Lizzie, really! The things you think of!"

"Well, how old is she, then?" I demanded.

"She's twenty-eight – nearly twenty-nine. Quite old enough, I assure you."

"But she's younger than Charles," I wailed. "How will he feel, having a mother-in-law who's younger than him?"

Daddy looked at me. "I'm sure he won't look at it like that. He likes Wendy a lot – so does Meg. We're hoping they'll be pleased for us."

"But what about Katey?" I persisted.

"What about her?" Daddy was clearly puzzled.

"You know – having a grandmother that age ..." I gestured helplessly.

"Lizzie," said Daddy gently, "do stop thinking about

Wendy's age. It really doesn't matter, you know. What matters is the fact we love each other, very much."

"Huh – love!" I muttered.

"Yes – love," he said firmly. "And she's very fond of you, too – don't you know that?"

"If she's that fond of me, why can't she see that I'm perfectly happy with things the way they are?" I asked, my voice rising again. "Why can't you leave things as they are – why've you got to *marry* her?" A sob cracked my voice.

"Lizzie," he said, taking my hands. "Lizzie, look at me."

"No," I said. I'd start to cry if I did: I knew I would.

"All right – just listen to me, then. I love Wendy – don't scoff, Lizzie. I want to marry her; it's only right and proper that I should."

"Why?" I interrupted.

Daddy sighed.

"It's something you'll understand when you get older, I promise you. I can't explain it to you now."

That seemed a cop-out to me. Daddy may have thought so too, because he tried to continue.

"It's just something that grown-ups feel when they're together ..." he trailed off lamely.

"D'you mean having babies, and all that stuff?" I asked. Daddy sort of half nodded.

"Something like that," he said.

"Is Miss Bullock having a baby, then?" I demanded.

"Good heavens no! – no, she's not," said Daddy hurriedly. I took my hands away from his.

"Besides," Daddy continued, "we thought it would be nice for you, too. You need a mother's influence."

I stood up quickly.

"I had a mother!" I was shouting again. "She died – remember?"

As soon as I said it I felt guilty. Daddy looked drained and defeated.

"Sit down, Lizzie. Please don't say things like that." So I sat down on the bed again.

"Now then," he said quietly. "We *are* getting married, and I'm sorry, but you've just got to get used to the idea. Anyway," he continued, his voice brightening, "you'll love it in London – your new school is the best in the area – and think of how easy it'll be to get to all the concerts and things!"

I stared at him. I couldn't have heard him correctly – London? What did he mean? I tried to speak, but no sound was coming out.

'What – what did you say?" I managed to croak.

"Didn't we tell you last night?" said Daddy, confused. "I thought we had. You must have rushed off before we had the chance."

"Tell me what?" I said; but I had a horrid feeling I knew what was coming.

"We'll be moving to London," said Daddy brightly. "It's so much more convenient – near my publisher – and the BBC want to do some interviews – possibly even a series – didn't I tell you? I can't keep going up there from Cornwall – it's much too far. This'll be much more convenient," he repeated.

I felt numb. I couldn't speak. Move away from Cornwall? – it was unthinkable. Daddy was still prattling away. I wanted him to shut up.

"… and, as I said, the musical possibilities for you are wonderful. Say something, Lizzie!"

I couldn't: it was as though I'd lost the ability to speak. I opened my mouth, but no sound came out but a choking sob. Suddenly, I felt extremely sick. I stood up, and everything went blurred. I could dimly hear

Daddy, still talking to me.

"... you all right, sweetie? You've gone frightfully pale ... Lizzie!"

I rushed out of the room, down the stairs. I had to get outside. Everything would be all right, as long as I got outside. I grabbed my mackintosh from its peg by the door and ran out into the fresh air. Rufus followed me, barking joyfully, thinking I was taking him for an unscheduled walk. I could hear Daddy behind me, calling my name. Then I dimly heard Miss Bullock joining in. And Rufus, still barking furiously. The noise was awful; I had to get away from it.

I stumbled through the slush, up the cliff path. I felt as though I was wearing wellington boots, running through treacle - my legs were like lead. Rufus was still panting along behind me.

"Go home!" I said to him angrily. "Go away!" But he wouldn't.

After what seemed like an age, I got to the top of the cliff path. I was sure my lungs had burst. There was an awful pain in my chest - burning, stabbing. Then I was suddenly, violently sick. It went on for ages, and I had nobody to hold my head. It was ghastly. All the same, I was glad no one was there to see me. My eyes and nose were streaming.

I felt a little better after I'd been sick. I found an old packet of mints in my mac pocket - I sucked one, to get rid of the awful taste. Then I covered the sick with some snow. Rufus was already looking interestedly at it. That dog disgusts me at times.

I suddenly felt very cold and put on my mac, which I'd been clutching to me the whole time. It wasn't very warm, but it was better than nothing. My feet were soaking, and freezing cold. I looked down at them: in my rush to get out of the cottage, I'd left my bedroom slippers on. They were soaked through.

I sat down on the snow: my legs just sort of gave way. Rufus came and sat with me, and I put my arms round him. I sat there with one thought going round and round my head: I'm leaving Cornwall, I'm leaving Cornwall. Eventually, even that thought went away, and I just sat there. After about a century of this, I saw two small figures far below me, on the Platt. I could see that it was Daddy and Miss Bullock, even from this distance. They were calling me: their voices came to me on the wind, but not their words. It didn't matter. I wasn't going down to them, anyway.

Eventually, they gave up and went away – but not back to the cottage. They were walking in the direction of Penlorren. I remembered we were supposed to be going to lunch with Meg and Charles – they were obviously going without me.

For some ridiculous reason, this hurt me more than

anything. The salt tears began to flow down my face as I imagined them all at the vicarage, having a lovely lunch without me, glad I wasn't there to spoil their fun and their news. I sobbed and sobbed, unable to stop. Rufus licked the tears from my face.

At last I pulled myself together. I wiped my face with my hanky and had a good blow. Then I looked at my watch. It was still only twelve o' clock.

I was freezing – I couldn't stay here, on the cliff top. On the other hand, I couldn't face going back to the cottage. I decided to go and see Ben. He'll understand, I promised myself. But when I knocked on the Polkerris' door, there was no reply. I just didn't know what to do – I'd so banked on being able to pour my heart out to Ben.

Rufus and I wandered around the streets for a while, pointlessly. I was soaked and freezing, and my world was falling apart around me. I eventually decided I'd better go home. There was nowhere else for me to go – I couldn't even go to Meg's, because *They* were there. At least, that's what I supposed. But when I let myself into the cottage I heard the low mumble of voices, and the slam of the front door brought Daddy into the hall.

"Lizzie?" He came to me and put his hand on my shoulder. "Don't look so stricken, sweetie. Everything will be all right."

I stared stupidly at him. "Why aren't – I thought you were at Meg's," I managed to say. "I saw you walking over ..."

"We wouldn't have gone out and left you, not knowing where you were," he said. "We were out looking for you – we thought you might have gone that way."

"Oh," I said. I turned to go upstairs. I felt awful.

"Don't go," said Daddy. "Come in and talk to us. We need to sort things out."

"I can't," I said in a small voice. "I don't want to talk to you, Daddy. I don't want to talk to anyone. Please don't make me."

He looked upset, but didn't try to stop me climbing the stairs. I sat on my bed and looked at all my photograph albums. My life, my Cornish life, was spread out before me – Penwithin, Penlorren and the Strand – the cliffs and the fishing boats – the cottage, with a puppy Rufus on the front step. Meg and Charles' wedding, with a proud Daddy between the happy couple. And the only picture I had of my mother – taken when I was christened. A pretty, blonde, serenely smiling lady holding a screaming bundle in a white shawl. Me. Too young to remember.

I took the photo gently from the page which held it and stared into my mother's face, willing myself to remember more about her than I was able. I felt so guilty that I was beginning to forget what she looked like, what she *was* like.

"Oh Mummy," I whispered. "Oh my Mummy."

There was a knock at my bedroom door, and then another.

"Lizzie," came Ben's voice, "it's me." I opened the door at once, wiping the tears from my face.

"I came round to see you," I said accusingly, "but you were out!"

"We've just got back. I thought I'd come to say 'Happy New Year'; and your Dad told me – you know. I say – are you OK? You look awful."

"It *is* awful. Oh Ben – we're moving. To London. And they're getting married ... I don't want them to." To my embarrassment I started to cry again and sat down on the bed, to try and hide the tears.

Ben sat down next to me and made sympathetic grunting noises. After a bit, he put an awkward arm around my shoulders.

"Don't cry, Lizzie. Look – it'll be OK, I'm sure. I'll be able to stay with you in the holidays – and you'll be able to come back and stay with ..." His voice trailed off. He could tell it was useless.

He sighed. "I'm not helping, am I?"

I shook my head violently.

"D'you want me to go?"

I looked at him. His face was so well-meaning. He was my best friend. He couldn't do a thing to help me.

"I just want to be on my own. Sorry, Ben," I said sadly. "I'll see you out though. Thanks for coming." We went downstairs.

"Happy New Year, anyway. Oh, blast," he said as he saw my face. "What a stupid thing to say!" He dug his hands into his pockets and trudged off into the snow.

I suddenly very much wanted to see Meg. I could hear Daddy whistling in the kitchen, so I went in.

"Did Ben cheer you up?" Daddy asked, smiling. It seemed such a fatuous thing to say, I didn't even answer.

"If you don't mind," I said quietly, "I think I'd like to go and see my sister."

"Why don't you just pop in the other room to say hello to Wendy?" he said. "She was terribly worried about you, rushing off like that."

I couldn't care less about your precious Wendy, I thought. "All right," I said. I went into the sitting room. Miss Bullock was sitting there, smiling her kindly, feminine, sickly smile at me. On her lap, purring, sat Fishpaste – the traitor. I felt betrayed. I walked out of the room without saying a word.

"What's wrong *now*?" asked Daddy. He was beginning to sound a bit impatient.

"She's got my cat on her lap," I said in a frozen voice. "Tell her to put him down."

"Certainly not!" said Daddy crossly. "Whatever has got into you? - *your* sister, *your* cat! I know you've had a shock - and I'm truly sorry you were upset, believe me - but I think it's about time you stopped thinking about *your* feelings and started considering those of other people!" He was very angry.

"Jamie," said a soft voice. *She'd* come into the kitchen. "Not now. Don't shout at her - poor Lizzie, she's very upset." She put her hand down and patted Rufus on the head. He licked her wrist.

"I'm not 'poor Lizzie' - I'm perfectly all right now, thank you," I said in a controlled voice. "And please stop sucking up to my animals - you won't get me to like you through them, if that's what you're thinking."

"Lizzie!" said Daddy, outraged.

"It's all right Jamie," she said soothingly. I hated her - her reasonableness.

"I'm going to see Meg now," I said and let myself out of the cottage.

I was rather worried about how I'd find them: Meg and Charles, I mean. It seemed to me that everybody I loved best in the world - Daddy, Fishpaste, Rufus, even Ben - had turned against me in some way or, at least, couldn't understand why I was feeling the way I was.

But I needn't have worried. As soon as Meg opened the door I could see that she understood perfectly. I started to cry again. I didn't think I had any tears left - it amazed me that I was so full of water. Meg just let me cry on her. She put her arms round me. When I stopped, and pulled away from her to find my sodden hanky, I noticed her face was wet too.

What a way to spend New Year's Day! I felt absolutely worn out, and totally empty inside. After I'd told Meg and Charles everything that had happened, Charles gently asked me why I felt the way I did. It was difficult to put into words, but I tried.

I told him about Miss Bullock spoiling everything: how Daddy and I had been quite happy until she came along. And now we were leaving my beloved Cornwall ... I couldn't bear it. Yet more tears found their way out of the depths of me, hot and scalding. Then I told them I was worried about Rufus and Fishpaste. Cities were no place for animals - I'd heard Mrs Morris say so, dozens of times. They'd been born in Cornwall. They couldn't leave it for a dingy, grey and colourless place like London - where would they play? And what about my school? I didn't want to leave it, not now I'd just begun to settle down.

After I'd told them all this, they left me alone in the room, staring into the fire. They brought me some tea presently - I was surprised to discover how hungry I was.

Then Meg insisted I go to bed. I didn't want to - it was only seven o' clock - but she was very firm.

"You're worn out," she declared. "You need a nice long rest. You'll feel a bit better in the morning, I promise." I doubted it.

"What about Daddy?" I remembered. "He'll be expecting me home." Not that I wanted to go home.

"I've rung him," she said. "We'll run you back tomorrow. Now off you trot - Charles is making you a hot water bottle."

I fell into bed and closed my eyes. Everything was going round and round in my mind. I'll never get to sleep, I thought; not after what's happened today, not at this time in the evening. It's far too early to sleep.

The next thing I knew, it was morning.

9

My thirteenth Birthday

After that, things seemed to change subtly between Daddy and me. I can't really describe it: we would sort of snipe at each other, like Rufus does at Fishpaste when he's feeling frisky and keeps biting Rufus' tail. Only Daddy and I seemed to be doing it more or less all the time.

So far as Miss Bullock was concerned, I just tried to ignore her. It wasn't too difficult, what with school and choir practice and violin lessons and seeing Maudie and things. But I stayed out of the cottage as much as I could. For one thing, Miss Bullock seemed to be forever there, at weekends and evenings, making interminable wedding lists with Daddy. I don't know why she didn't just move a camp-bed in and stay.

The other reason I kept away was because Daddy was already starting to pack in readiness for moving to beastly London: wrapping up bits of my past in tissue-paper and packing them away in tea-chests. I couldn't stand this constant reminder that we were leaving Cornwall, and leaving quite soon. It seemed that *She* had had a hand in our projected move – I'd guessed as much.

Her parents live in Richmond, which is just outside London. Ben called it 'commuter land' when I told him – I don't really know what that means, I have to confess. The way Ben said it didn't make it sound very nice, though. Anyway, her parents were apparently giving her and Daddy a house for a wedding present – can you imagine it! A *house*! They must be as rich as Croesus. The house was in a place called Barnes, which isn't actually properly London but in the suburbs, as they're called. It's also near Richmond, which figures.

"It's quite countrified really," said Daddy when he was telling me. "There's a big common right behind the house – Rufus will love it. And it's very close to the river."

I was glad that Rufus and Fishpaste would be able to get their exercise properly, but I still wasn't at all happy with the arrangements.

"It's not Cornwall though," I said gloomily.

"No," said Daddy, sighing. "It's not Cornwall. But you'll enjoy it, if you'd only give yourself a chance. You seem to have shut your mind to the whole thing."

That wasn't true – my mind had shut automatically, with no help from me. I decided to try another tack.

"Why are her parents buying you a house?" I asked Daddy. "Can't you afford one?"

He laughed. "Yes, I should think we could – although London prices are a bit different to the ones down here. Especially in a place like Barnes. But they want to give it to us – and between you and me, I reckon it's a bit of a tax dodge."

"Are they very rich?" I asked.

"Very – Wendy's father is a self-made man, a millionaire. He's very big in the City, I gather."

"Are you marrying her for her money, then?" I asked him unkindly.

"Lizzie!" Daddy looked hurt. "What a thing to say!"

"I can't see you accepting a house from Granny and Grandad," I grumbled.

Daddy doesn't get on with his own parents, who live abroad. They're my only grandparents: my mother's parents died when she was a little girl.

"Granny and Grandad wouldn't offer – although they're not short of a bob or two, either," he said. "And I wouldn't accept, even if they did offer."

"Then why *are* you marrying her if it's not the money?" I didn't really mean it – I just wondered what he'd say. He was cross, but tried not to let it show.

"I've told you already," he said in mock-patient tones. "Why won't you even try to understand, Lizzie?"

"Oh yes, I forgot – 'love', wasn't it?" I said sulkily. He lost his temper.

"What's the matter with you? You've turned into a horrible little girl! I didn't even *know* about her father's money until after I'd proposed to her!" he said, his voice rising angrily.

The "horrible little girl" bit stung me. That was the problem – I wasn't a little girl any more; I was nearly grown up, but they still treated me and thought of me as being a child. They didn't realise I had feelings on the matter; they just presented me with it. "Here you are," they were saying, "here's your new mother. Mind you love her, now, like you did the old one!" But I couldn't. I couldn't even think of Miss Bullock as becoming Daddy's wife, let alone my mother – albeit a stepmother.

The wedding was planned for Easter Saturday. It was to be in London, with the reception in a huge marquee on her parents' lawn. Typical, I thought scornfully. I was already beginning to think of her parents as being flashy, ostentatious people.

We were all to drive up from Cornwall two days before the wedding, on Maundy Thursday. Then on Easter Sunday, after the wedding, *She* and Daddy would go off on their honeymoon and I would drive back with Meg and Charles to spend the rest of the Easter holidays with them at the vicarage. After that ... I didn't want to think about after that.

Trust her to want to get married at Easter, I pondered. Charles was having terrible problems getting leave of absence for the wedding: Easter, along with Christmas, being a clergyman's busiest time of year. He was practically having to write a personal letter to God to ask for the time off. I was praying that something would happen to stop it all taking place. So far, God didn't seem to be answering my prayers.

I was going to be a bridesmaid. I'd never been one before - when Meg and Charles got married, not long after the Awful Time, they hadn't had any bridesmaids: I'd played a violin solo instead - and I must confess to a reluctant excitement at the thought of being one. When they'd asked me, though, it had ended up with Daddy getting cross again.

"Will you be our bridesmaid, Lizzie? - do say you will! We'd love you to," *She* had said, eyes shining. Silly bag, I thought.

"I'm not bothered," I replied offhandedly.

"Lizzie!" said Daddy warningly.

"Well, I'm not," I said.

"And why not, may I ask? Most girls your age would jump at the chance to be a bridesmaid."

"Not at their *father*'s weddings," I said. I wanted to stop, but couldn't. "Most girls' my age fathers are already married - to people their own age," I added as an afterthought.

So Daddy yelled at me again and said I was an ungrateful little brat. *She* tried to calm him down. She seemed to be doing a lot of that lately. I should have thought it would put her off, seeing what a temper he had, and what horrid things he was capable of calling his beloved daughter (i.e. me). But it didn't seem to.

The time creaked by, and then it was March, and my birthday. I was to be thirteen – a teenager. And the wedding was only a month away. My life seemed to have changed drastically in the year since my last birthday.

This year, my birthday was on a Sunday. Daddy had to go and see a man at the BBC on the Saturday, so they had this great idea that we should all go to London together for the weekend. At least, *they* thought it was great. I thought it was pretty dire, the idea of being stuck with them both for the whole weekend, until they said Maudie could come too. That cheered me up a bit, though Maudie got on my nerves by being so enthusiastic about the whole thing. The idea was that we should go off and buy my bridesmaid's dress while Daddy was at the BBC. Then we would stay overnight with *Her* old college friend, Grace, and travel back to Cornwall some time on the Sunday. Grace was also going to be a bridesmaid and would come with us to choose her bridesmaid's dress. She and her husband had a flat in Putney, which is near the dreaded Barnes. Miss Bullock got quite excited when she'd made these plans. She said to Daddy, "We can take Lizzie to see the house on Sunday now, Jamie." Daddy muttered something I couldn't hear and frowned in my general direction. I don't think he thought it a very good idea.

We caught a very early train on the Saturday morning and arrived in London at lunchtime. Grace was there to meet us at Paddington. She was small and very pretty, with bobbed dark hair. She was dressed in vivid colours and reminded me of someone. Then I realized who it was – me! She was much older, and prettier, but we definitely looked alike.

Grace noticed it too.

"Good heavens, Lizzie!" she said. "You could be my sister!" Then she looked sideways at Miss Bullock. "Trust Wendy to have matching bridesmaids," she said shrewdly. I decided I liked her.

We went on the Underground to Oxford Circus. It was hot and smelt dusty, and was full of hurrying harassed-looking shoppers and tourists. When we emerged into daylight again, Daddy went off to Broadcasting House, and we all went to an Italian restaurant.

We ate pizzas and drank Coke, and Maudie wriggled excitedly on her seat. She'd never been to London before. Neither had I, I have to admit – except once, when I was just a baby. Sitting in London now, the day before my thirteenth birthday, I must confess I was excited despite myself. I tried to hide it though: I didn't want *Her* to think she was getting round me. I was glad Maudie was with me, to give me moral support. Though she was scarcely an ally – she tended to suck up to Miss Bullock the way Fishpaste and Rufus had started to do. It was cupboard-love with them, though, I comforted myself. I don't know what it was with Maudie.

After we'd eaten, we went to a Laura Ashley shop. It had frocks in both Grace's and my sizes, and we tried on a few. Then Miss Bullock came into my changing-room holding another one.

"Try this," she said, "I think this is the one."

It was so pretty. I have to say it. It was a sea-green floral print. The neckline was sort of heart-shaped and the sleeves were short, ending at the elbow, and very puffed. There were yards and yards of calf-length skirt, ending in a deep frill, and a wide sash around the middle. I looked at myself in the mirror and pulled faces.

"Don't!" said Maudie who was in there with me. "It looks lovely – don't spoil it."

She was right – it *did* look lovely. It made me look curious: older *and* younger, both at the same time. I pulled the curtain aside and went out.

There in front of me stood Grace, in a larger and longer version of the same dress. For a moment we stood there staring solemnly at each other. It was a bizarre feeling: like looking at myself in a distorted mirror. Then Grace started to laugh. She grabbed my hand and skipped about, singing 'She's getting married in the morning.' I couldn't help laughing too. It was very infectious.

Miss Bullock bought the dresses. After seeing those, we couldn't imagine anything else looking as nice. We went to some more shops: Miss Bullock bought a white hat, 'for going away in.' This wretched wedding seemed to be becoming more and more real. I didn't like it.

We spent the rest of the afternoon walking in the early spring sunshine in Regent's Park. I was surprised that there was so much green right in the middle of London. And a zoo – I was enthralled.

"I'll take you there soon – in the summer holidays, if you like," said Miss Bullock.

For a moment, I nearly forgot myself. "Oh, yes please," I started to say. Then I remembered. "I expect I'll be too busy to go to the zoo" I said loftily. "Anyway, I'll be in Cornwall for the holidays."

We duly met Daddy at the BBC and then caught a bus to Putney. I was beginning to wonder how Grace would manage to fit four extra people into her flat overnight – I was imagining a small flat, like Miss Bullock had in Cornwall. But when I saw it, I was amazed. It was huge, like a mansion, with four vast bedrooms. We met Grace's husband Joshua – he was nice, too. He told us he was an accountant. Grace called him Josh. He was tall and fair, with twinkling green eyes: I could see Maudie was finding it difficult to keep her heart true to Mr Trotter when she talked to Joshua. She fluttered around like a butterfly.

Grace made a great panful of spaghetti bolognaise for supper and we had green salad and garlic bread. They all drank red wine from a bottle with straw round it. Maudie and I watched TV in the study while they talked in the dining room.

At nine o' clock, Grace came in and asked us if we were ready for bed. We were both exhausted after the early start we'd had that morning, so we didn't mind. It seemed funny not going upstairs to bed – and not having Fishpaste sleeping on my tummy. Meg was looking after the animals at the vicarage for the weekend.

Something woke me up suddenly, in the middle of the night. I looked at the luminous hands of the clock: half past twelve. It was my birthday. Then I heard voices – Miss Bullock's and Daddy's voices. I climbed out of bed and stood by the door, listening. They were arguing. I listened in amazement.

"... too soft with her. She's acting like a spoilt brat," I heard Daddy say.

"She wasn't like that today. The front came down, several times. She'll come round, you'll see," said Miss

Bullock. With a shock, I realised they were talking about me. I listened hard for more, but their voices became indistinct. Then I heard Daddy's again, raised in anger.

"That's just the trouble! She's *not* your daughter! If she were, she'd be spoilt rotten!"

"That's not fair, James!" I heard Miss Bullock retort. James! She'd called him James, instead of her usual Jamie! She *must* be cross, I thought.

"She's hurt and upset, and reacting accordingly. It's no use going at her like a bull at a gate – that'll just antagonise her even more."

I nodded in agreement with Miss Bullock's words without realizing I was doing so.

"Oh yes – *you're* the bloody expert on kids, aren't you," said Daddy sarcastically.

"No – I'm no expert," she replied. "But I've seen enough of them at school in this situation to know how Lizzie's feeling at the moment." Oh no, you don't, I thought – *nobody* does. I gulped self-pityingly. But Daddy hadn't finished.

"Is that why you want to marry me, then – to take on my child, have a ready-made family, as you can't have any of your own?" There was a silence. I was trying to work out what Daddy meant. Then Miss Bullock spoke again – very slowly and quietly. I could barely hear her.

"That's a rotten, hurtful thing to sling at me," she said. "If that's what you think, perhaps we're doing the wrong thing in getting married."

"Perhaps we are," said Daddy.

I held my breath.

"Perhaps we should call the whole thing off," she said.

"Perhaps we should," he agreed.

There was another long pause. Then: "I think you ought to go to bed," said Miss Bullock. "We're both tired." Then the voices went back to murmurs again. I heard footsteps outside the bedroom door and slid back to bed, shivering. They've argued, I thought. They've been arguing. Strangely, the thought brought me no joy at all.

But the next day – my birthday – they were back to being friends again. Sickeningly so – they held hands under the table all through breakfast. It quite put me off my Weetabix.

It was odd, having my birthday in a strange house – or rather, flat – without my animals, or Meg and Charles, being there. Everybody seemed to have gone mad on the idea of me being thirteen and had bought me grown-up things. Maudie gave me some make-up – eyeshadow and blusher and stuff. Daddy frowned rather when he saw it, but Miss Bullock said "What fun! We can have a beauty session!"

Miss Bullock gave me a white broderie anglaise nightie. It must have cost the earth. I thanked her politely and put it to one side. The nicest present was from Daddy. He gave me a gold cross and chain, to wear around my neck. It was lovely. Then he said, "You can wear it for the wedding", and I suddenly went off it.

After breakfast, Joshua took us in his huge car to see that house at Barnes. Barnes is a good name for it: the house seemed like a barn. It was enormous. Bigger than Charles' vicarage. It had a long, rambling garden which backed onto the Common. At least Rufus would be able to rush around, I thought, and Fishpaste could hide in the laurel. It was the only good thing I could find to think about it. The house stood there largely, reminding me that I was soon to live there instead of my beautiful Cornwall.

I was beginning to feel rather odd. Everyone had gone to look upstairs and I was on my own in the garden. Suddenly, Grace was there with me. She looked at me anxiously.

"What's the matter, chicken?" she said. "Don't you feel well?" Understanding began to dawn on her face. "They never asked you how *you* felt about this, did they?" she said.

I shook my head miserably.

"Try not to mind too much," she said softly. "You'll settle down – just you wait and see. Anyway," she went on, grinning, "you can always come and cry on my shoulder if things get too much. I'm only just up the road."

"Can I?" I said. I had a feeling I'd need an ally – and, despite the fact that she was Miss Bullock's friend, I had the distinct impression she *was* my ally in all this.

"Course you can – any time," she said. "Come on – they're coming downstairs."

Together, we walked up the overgrown garden to the house.

10

The Wedding

*D*ear Diary,   *20th April.*
I am writing this in Her *parents' house in Richmond.*
We drove down this afternoon. In two days' time, they
will be married. I wish I could make time stand still.
Daddy has been busy selling the cottage – we've had
hordes of horrid grockles looking round and saying it's
too small. I hoped we wouldn't be able to sell it – but we
did. I can't bear the thought of never going back there ...
I can't write any more, I'm too upset. I really hate Daddy
at times.

I'd persuaded Daddy to let me bring Rufus to London
with us for the wedding – although he wasn't going to at
first – but all my entreaties couldn't budge him about
Fishpaste. He had to stay in Cornwall, being looked after
(rather reluctantly) by Mrs Morris. Everybody else – apart
from Maudie who was in Scotland for Easter – was
coming to the wedding. Charles had finally got
permission from God for the time off – I'd driven with
him and Meg up to Richmond (I couldn't face the
thought of that long journey with Daddy and *Her*).

Mrs Morris had been invited, but had courteously declined the invitation. "It's me legs, see," she said, with a loud sniff. "They'd never be up to all that standing around, nattering, like." But she'd given them a very nice set of fish knives as a wedding present.

All Ben's family were attending the wedding: Mrs Polkerris' sister was looking after the shop. They were all staying in a very swish hotel in Richmond – *Her* family were paying. This wedding must be costing them a bomb, I thought. But they looked as though they could afford it.

Their house – I've never seen anything like it. I thought we'd taken the wrong turning and gone to a stately home when we arrived. Big doesn't describe it adequately – it was much, much bigger than simply 'big'. Charles chuckled when he saw it. Meg was goggle-eyed – so was I.

It was like a stately home inside, too – full of antiquey-looking furniture. I was afraid of breaking something. A maid in a white cap and apron took our things upstairs. I was in the 'Lilac Room' – it was all decorated in guess what? – yes, lilac. It *was* very pretty. I had my own washbasin in the room, with stacks and stacks of lilac and clover-coloured towels. I'll have to have a lot of baths to get through that lot, I thought.

There was an electric kettle on a tray with tea-making things and – best of all – a tin of chocolate biscuits. I knew I'd be able to sneak Rufus up later and we could have a midnight feast.

Ordinarily, all this would have delighted me but I was filled with gloom at the reason why we were here. The maid had unpacked all my things and laid them on the bed. I put them all back in the suitcase, except the bridesmaid's dress which I carefully hung up in the wardrobe. Then I washed my face and hands, and went in search of Meg and Charles.

We went downstairs in a solemn band to meet Mr and Mrs Bullock. (She's really the Hon. Mrs Bullock – it said so on the invitations.) Daddy and Miss Bullock were just arriving.

"Hello, Mummy," said Miss Bullock.

I couldn't believe my ears – fancy still calling her mother "Mummy" at her age! Mrs Bullock didn't look like anyone's Mummy – she looked more like a governess, or a crusty great-aunt.

Rufus came wriggling in, nearly knocking a vase over with his tail.

"Take that dawg to the kitchen!" boomed Mrs Bullock to the maid.

"Leave him be, Constance," said her husband. He had a Yorkshire accent. "He's just excited – he'll settle down."

Then Meg and Charles and I were introduced.

"Hello, Mr Bullock," I said. He smiled widely and kissed my hand.

"Ah, the youngest bridesmaid, I presume." He was jolly. If he hadn't been *Her* father, I'd really have liked him. Then his wife held out her hand.

"Elizabeth, isn't it?" she said, peering at me over the top of spectacles.

"Lizzie," said Daddy hastily. "We all call her Lizzie."

"I shall call her Elizabeth," she announced to the room. "I cannot abide abbreviations of names. That's why our daughter was christened Wendy – one cannot shorten it."

"I was saying that to Wen the other day," whispered Charles in my ear. I wanted to laugh, but instead took her outstretched hand.

"How do you do, Honourable Mrs Bullock," I said

politely. They all burst out laughing. Mr Bullock was laughing louder than anybody. He wiped his eyes.

"Well, at least she didn't shorten *your* name, Constance," he wheezed.

I still don't know what I'd said that was so funny.

The next day dawned, wet and windy. It suited my mood. I stared out of the window at the lowering clouds and felt utterly miserable at the thought of the events tomorrow was to bring. Some men were trying to erect a flapping marquee on the lawn, just at the point where it began to slope down to the river. They weren't having much success: the whole thing looked as if it was going to take off at any second. I'm glad it's raining, I thought – I hope it pours and pours all day tomorrow. That'll spoil it.

But the rain eased off by mid-morning, and Daddy dragged us all off to Richmond Park. We saw some deer, but only in the distance. Rufus charged around chasing sticks. It started to rain again; it was going down my neck. I hunched up my shoulders inside my mac. Everybody else was ignoring the rain – they were playing an elaborate game of piggy-in-the-middle, with Rufus as the piggy, barking ecstatically. They were all rosy-cheeked and laughing.

"What's the matter, Lizzie?" Daddy called to me. How can he pretend not to know? – I thought. I ignored him.

"Hi, Lizzie! Come and be the pig!" shouted Charles.

"She'd be good at that – she's been practising being a pig just lately," said Daddy, laughing.

I'd had enough. I called to Rufus: the wretched dog ignored me.

"Where are you going?" called Meg.

"Home," I yelled.

"What – all the way to Cornwall?" shouted Daddy.

There was a silence. I think they then realised what was up.

"I wish I could – I hate you all!" I bawled dramatically and ran off. My exit was spoiled rather by tripping over a large clump of grass, but I picked myself up and carried on. I could hardly see where I was going. As I let myself into the house, I literally ran into Mr Bullock.

"Steady now – steady!" he said. I pushed upstairs past him and locked myself in the Lilac Room.

I was expecting them all to come after me, but they didn't. After about an hour, I heard them all come back. I was getting rather bored by myself. I heard Meg and Charles come laughing up the stairs. I wanted to open my door, to go sauntering into their room as though nothing had happened, but somehow I just couldn't.

"I'll show them," I muttered to myself. I managed to squeeze a few tears out.

Charles eventually came and tapped on my door. "Lunch, Lizzie," he said cheerfully.

"Don't want any," I said sulkily.

"What?" he said, through the door.

"I said, I don't want any. Go away!" I shouted.

There was a pause. Then: "Oh. All right then," he said.

I heard them all go downstairs. I was amazed! They're going to leave me here, on my own without any lunch! I thought incredulously.

All afternoon I sat there on my own. I was starving, but I wasn't going to give in. I'll show them, I kept saying to myself.

At about half past four, there was another tap at the door. I didn't answer and presently heard footsteps going away, so I cautiously opened the door. There on the floor was a tray, with some ham sandwiches and a chocolate éclair on a bone china plate. There was also a note, in Meg's handwriting: "Dinner tonight at 7.30. *Be there.*" I considered ignoring the note, but thought better of it: I was still hungry, despite the sandwiches. I decided to go down to dinner, but that I would stay utterly silent. I wouldn't talk to anyone - not *anyone*, I told myself firmly. Then they'll see how I feel. Then they will be sorry ...

Dinner that evening was a hilarious affair, full of excited chatter, for everybody but me. Grace and Joshua had arrived that afternoon and Grace tried to talk to me, but I ignored her along with everybody else. Nobody made much of an effort to make me talk, I must say - it was a bit of a let-down.

After dinner, when everybody left the table, I decided to go to bed. I could write my diary up in peace, telling it how horrid everybody had been to me today. But Meg walked up the stairs behind me: at the top, she held on to my arm and said, "Come into our room for a moment." I didn't think to say no - she sounded so serious.

"Sit down," she said.

I sat on the bed.

"Now then," she said. "I've got to say this to you, because I doubt if anyone else will."

"Say what to me?" I asked, mystified.

"Oh, hooray - you *have* got a tongue, then?" she said sarcastically. Meg was never sarcastic - I stared at her. Her expression softened and she sat on the bed next to me.

"Listen, Lizzie," she said, "we all know you're not keen on this wedding, and the move and everything, and we're all sorry for you. We know how you feel - really we do - nobody means to hurt you."

"Yes, you do," I blazed, jumping up. "Nobody understands – everybody's against me! Well, I'm not going to the wedding: I'll – I'll – I'll lock myself in my room all day!"

A dark cloud passed over her face. She looked very stern and un-Meg-like.

"Listen to me," she said. "We are all trying very hard to be sympathetic to you, but you're not making it very easy for us. You will *not* lock yourself in your room – you will not do anything so childish. You will go to this wedding, and what's more, you will behave yourself. Because I'll tell you this," she pushed her face close to mine and wagged her finger. "If you do anything – *anything* at all – to spoil Daddy's day, I'll never forgive you. Do you understand?"

I nodded, mesmerised.

"Good." She kissed my cheek. "Now go to bed."

As I put on my bridesmaid's dress the next day, I felt a reluctant excitement growing inside me.

"Isn't this fun?" laughed Grace. She was getting changed in the Lilac Room with me: the bedroom she and Joshua had been given to sleep in was being used by the ushers as a changing-room. Joshua was the chief usher.

When we were ready, we regarded each other gravely. We did look nice – as well as wearing the dresses, we had circlets of fresh flowers in our newly-done hair and white satin ballet slippers on our feet. I was carrying a Victorian posy of flowers – all white ones, roses and freesias and carnations – and Grace had a larger version. I hardly recognised myself when I looked in the mirror.

"Come on," said Grace, "we'd better go and view the bride before we leave – the car's here."

Miss Bullock had her back to us when we walked into

her room. Then she turned round. I nearly fell over in amazement. She looked – beautiful, I suppose. That's the only word. Her dress was a similar style to ours, only more so – more skirt, more sleeves, and a train. Her blonde hair was simply caught up on top, and a full-length, satin-trimmed veil was held in place by a larger version of our flower circlets. She was carrying a huge bouquet of flowers, the biggest I've ever seen. It went down to the ground in tendrils of ivy and fern and carnations, and the scent coming from it was heavenly.

But the most beautiful thing about Miss Bullock was her face. It was shining with joy, as if she'd just seen the most beautiful thing in the world. For a moment I had the strangest feeling. Then I remembered I wasn't supposed to be enjoying the day, and Grace and I went downstairs to get in the car.

Mrs Bullock was flapping about, trying to organize people.

"Get in the car and go to the church, Constance," said Mr Bullock patiently. He was dressed in one of those fancy coats that are short in the front and long at the back, with grey striped trousers and waistcoat. Morning dress, it's called. I don't know why – it was nearly quarter to two in the afternoon!

"Be sure to give people orange juice if they prefer," she said to a hired maid. The maid bobbed a curtsey. Mrs Bullock turned to her husband.

"Oh, Gordon," she said. She suddenly looked smaller, as though all the air had been let out of her. "Oh, Gordon ..." He patted her shoulder kindly.

"Just leave everything to me. I'll make sure Wendy gets there on time: don't you fret." She smiled at him, and looked human again. Then we got into the big black limousine and drove off.

At the church, Daddy and Charles had just arrived. Charles was being Daddy's best man. They were both wearing the same sort of clothes as Mr Bullock, and carrying pale grey top hats and gloves. Daddy had a white rose in his buttonhole. He looked very handsome. I had a lump in my throat. He saw us arriving and came over to us, as we scrunched up the gravel path to the church.

"Lizzie," he said, taking my hands. "You look gorgeous, sweetie."

"So do you," I replied truthfully. His hands were shaking. "Are you all right, Daddy?"

"I'm fine – just nervous. Isn't that ridiculous?" I reached up and gave him a kiss.

"That's for luck," I said. I didn't add, You'll need it. To be honest, I didn't even think it.

"You'll try and enjoy today, won't you?" he asked anxiously. I could see it was important to him.

"Of course I will," I said bravely. For your sake, Daddy, not Her's, I thought.

Inside the cool, flower-bedecked church, the organist was playing suitable waiting-for-the-bride music. The car with Meg, Joshua and the other ushers arrived. Then the guests began to turn up. The sun miraculously came out and the clouds blew away, and when the white Rolls-Royce carrying Miss Bullock and her father arrived, it was a lovely spring afternoon. As she stepped out of the car, the photographer rushed forward in a flurry of clicks. Mrs Bullock organized the photographer, until Mr Bullock said, "Do go and sit down, Constance, so we can be off." He made it sound like a horse race.

At last, we were all ready and waiting in the porch. There was a breathless pause; then the organist struck up 'Here comes the Bride.' I could hear a rustle from inside the church as everybody stood up, then 'oohs' and 'aahs' as Miss Bullock slowly walked up the aisle on her father's arm. The church was very old and very small, and it was packed. I could see Daddy at the chancel steps, looking down the aisle at us. He was smiling and I smiled back. Then I realised he was smiling at Miss Bullock, not me. When we reached the chancel steps, he gave her a look of melting tenderness. It was as though they were the only two people in the church. I felt quite strange for a moment. Then I realised she was passing me her bouquet to hold, so I had to pay attention.

It's an odd feeling, being a bridesmaid at your father's wedding. Although I must say it was a lovely service – I tried hard to concentrate on that, rather than the people concerned. When the vicar said that bit about if there's any man present who knows any just cause or impediment, blah blah, let him now speak or else hereafter forever hold his peace, I held my breath. I half-hoped someone at the back of the church would shout out that she had a husband and six children at home – but nobody did. I was quite relieved in a way – it would have been such a waste of all that lovely food waiting in the marquee.

During the signing of the register, another college friend of Miss Bullock's sang part of *Exsultate Jubilate* by Mozart. It's glorious: just the word "Allelujah" over and over again, but the music is wonderful. When we all walked back down the aisle, the organist played Widor's Toccata. I love it – I want that at my wedding. If I ever get married, that is.

Afterwards, we stood in the sunshine outside the church and all the bells were ringing and everybody was talking at once. Daddy and Miss Bullock stood in the porch, their arms around each other, their faces

wreathed in adoring smiles. I felt a pang of desolation –
it was done. She was his wife. Then I forced the thought
from my mind. I had promised Meg and Daddy I would
try and enjoy myself. Besides, all that food would cheer
me up – and the champagne.

There were interminable photographs outside the
church. My smile muscles were beginning to ache –
goodness knows how Miss Bullock and Daddy must
have felt. Ben came over to talk to me. He stared at me
in my bridesmaid's dress.

"What's the matter?" I asked him. "Don't you think I
look nice?"

"Yes, you do," he replied thoughtfully, "but you don't
look like you."

"What?" – it was gibberish to me. How could I not
look like me?

Finally, all the photos done, we piled into the cars and
went back to the house, and the marquee. The marquee
was decorated inside with swags of white flowers and
greenery. There was a string quartet playing in the
corner. I wandered over and looked over the viola
player's shoulder until he got fed up and told me to buzz
off. Cheek – they weren't that good, anyway. Then I said
hello to various aunts and uncles I hadn't seen for ages
and they made the inevitable observations about how
much I'd grown since they saw me last. I do think it's
ridiculous when relatives say that: imagine if you stayed
the same size all your life! There'd be an awful lot of
small people around.

The noise of people talking and laughing was almost
unbearable. Ben and I were eyeing the food hungrily, but
at last, the toastmaster clapped his hands and announced
"The Bride and Groom – Mr and Mrs Oliver." Another
pang went through me at that – I could never think of

her as Mrs Oliver, never. Mummy was Mrs Oliver, and always would be. Meg caught my eye – she looked a bit downcast, too.

Then we started the food; it was delicious. You could eat everything with your fingers, so didn't need a fork. Everything was in bite-sized pieces. There were vol-au-vents, and smoked salmon, and caviar – I didn't like that much, despite the fact people make so much fuss about it. There were tiny strawberry tartlets, and meringues, and éclairs, and sticky nutty chocolatey biscuits called florentines.

At last, Daddy and Miss Bullock cut the four-tier wedding cake, amid much applause. Then we had champagne, and speeches. I didn't really listen to them – I find speeches, like sermons, deadly dull – but at one point in Daddy's he said, "And I'd like to thank my younger daughter Lizzie for all the love, help and care she's given me, especially in recent difficult years." Everybody looked at me, and clapped and murmured. I felt myself go scarlet with embarrassment – and shame, too. I couldn't help thinking I hadn't shown Daddy much love or care in the past few months.

Then it was Charles' turn, to make the Best Man's speech. Everybody started laughing and pointing to the entrance of the marquee. Rufus came lolloping in, tongue hanging out, looking pleased with himself. He had a huge white satin bow round his neck, and tied to it were all the telegrams. I was pleased somebody had thought to include him in the celebrations. When Charles had freed him of the telegrams, Rufus came over to me and I fed him with wedding cake.

After all this, Daddy and Miss Bullock went round the reception to talk to everybody. People were admiring Miss Bullock's dress. Someone said to Daddy, "Such a shame your parents couldn't make it to the wedding," to which Daddy replied, with a snort, "Wouldn't, more like!"

Eventually, he and Miss Bullock disappeared into the house, "to get changed to go away, I expect," said Ben's Mum. While they were getting changed, Charles and Joshua and a few others decorated the hired car Daddy had driven up from Cornwall. They sprayed it with shaving foam and wrapped about three unravelled toilet rolls around it. It looked a right mess when they'd finished, I can tell you.

When the bride and groom reappeared, Daddy was in an ordinary suit, and Miss Bullock was in an outfit the same sea-green as the bridesmaids' dresses, topped with the white hat she'd bought in London the day before my birthday. They got into the car, accompanied by much cheering and throwing of confetti. I could see their luggage in the back: it was all new. I'd helped Daddy buy it before Christmas, little knowing what it was intended for. Then they drove off, tin cans rattling behind them. People cheered and waved, and then straggled back to the marquee, laughing and chattering.

Rufus and I were left alone in the drive. I was still waving long after the car had disappeared from sight. I knew that, once I stopped waving, they'd be gone. Rufus suddenly whined. The sound did something to me; I stopped waving and burst into tears.

Then Charles was there, behind me.

"Poor little Lizzie," he said, handing me a hanky. "Don't stop – cry it all out. You'll feel better for it."

I couldn't stop, even if I'd wanted to. Seeing Daddy and Miss Bullock driving off into the sunset confirmed the fact that my old life was finally, irrevocably over. And I knew with a crushing certainty that the new one wouldn't suit me at all.

PART TWO
London

1

Barnes

As I sat in the back of Charles' car, I pretended to be asleep. That way, Meg and Charles wouldn't talk to me and I wouldn't have to answer them. I didn't feel up to making conversation, even with them.

I was being taken to my new life. Daddy and Miss Bullock had got back from their Italian honeymoon earlier in the week, and Charles had told Daddy that he would ensure my safe arrival in London.

So here I was, being ferried across the country like a refugee with all my possessions, and Rufus and Fishpaste. It was kind of Charles, but I could get no comfort from his kindness. I was leaving the place that had been home to me for as long as I could remember, and I was sunk in misery.

As we sped through the English countryside, heading eastwards, I reflected on the events which had happened after the wedding. I'd gone back to Cornwall with Meg and Charles, as arranged, to spend the rest of the Easter holidays with them at the vicarage, and an extra week on top of that.

Those weeks had simply flown by. I spent them with Ben and Maudie. Everything we did seemed to have a special significance: the last time I would ever visit the Strand, or accompany Maudie's erratic recorder playing, or go to choir practice.

"But you'll be back, won't you – for holidays?" asked Maudie anxiously.

"It won't be the same, though; I'll be a visitor then, a grockle," I replied sadly.

Exactly a week after the wedding Ben's Mum and Dad took us to St Michael's Mount for the day – Ben and his sisters, Maudie, Rufus and me. I thought it rather odd at the time. Saturday is usually the busiest day in the Polkerris' shop and here they were, leaving it in the care of Mrs Polkerris' sister for the second week running. But I put it down to them trying to cheer me up, as everybody had seemed to be doing since the wedding. I'm not altogether sure it was the best way to treat me, to be honest. Everybody was making such a huge effort to be nice to me, not to upset me, that it was almost impossible for me to forget about things and just enjoy my last weeks in Cornwall. But I wouldn't have admitted that to anyone – they were only trying to be kind. Anyway, we had a gorgeous day out at St Michael's Mount, and when we got back to Penwithin, Mr Polkerris parked the car at the top of the village as usual and we all climbed out. I was staying for supper; then Meg and Charles were walking over to collect me and take me back to the vicarage.

We walked a funny way back to the shop – we avoided going past the cottage, my old home. I thought that odd, too, but put it down to the elaborate tiptoeing around my feelings they were all doing: "if Lizzie sees the cottage she'll be upset."

Charles and Meg collected me at about eight o'clock. This time, we went the normal way – but, as we approached the cottage, Rufus began to bark. Then I noticed – there were lights on, one shining through the kitchen window, and another upstairs.

"Charles!" I said, alarmed. "Look! Lights, in the cottage! It must be burglars!"

The cottage had stood empty since the day we left for Richmond, before the wedding: empty, that is, except for the furniture and the remainder of our possessions, Daddy's and mine, piled into tea-chests in the kitchen.

Charles and Meg exchanged glances. Rufus carried on barking menacingly.

"Come on!" I said, making for the front door. "We'd better see what's happening. Rufus will chase them off!"

"No, Lizzie," said Meg hastily. "Come back! Oh, Rufus, do shut up!" Rufus obediently stopped, in mid-woof.

"Let's get back to the vicarage," said Charles, taking my arm and hurrying me past. "We'll explain everything then – it's all right, honestly," as I stopped and looked back over my shoulder. I couldn't understand what was happening.

But it all became clear when we got back to the vicarage. Charles explained that the removal men had come today, to pack all the furniture and stuff into their van and take it to the house in Barnes. Charles had organized things this end.

"Wendy's parents met them the other end," he explained, "to make sure it was all unloaded properly. We spoke to them on the phone about an hour ago. Everything's fine, so you needn't worry," he assured me.

That's when I started to feel like an immigrant. My home was being moved around me, my possessions ...

"My things!" I cried. "My violin – and my music! And

my books - and my clothes! Where are they all - what have you done with them?"

"It's all right," soothed Meg. "We've left everything you brought here upstairs - we haven't touched any of that. And we brought the rest of your clothes and books over, in the trunk - that's upstairs too."

"We'll take that with us when we take you home next week," said Charles.

Home! - they were calling that horrible barn of a house 'home'. It would never be home to me. Then it suddenly dawned on me - the purpose of the trip today, my lovely day out to St Michael's Mount.

"You were getting rid of me for the day," I said slowly, accusingly. "You just wanted me out of the way so I wouldn't realise what was going on - you weren't going to tell me, were you?"

"Of course we were, Lizzie," said Meg gently. "It wasn't like that - we weren't trying to fool you, honestly."

"We just didn't want to upset you," explained Charles. "It would have been awful for you to see all your things being packed up and driven off - we wanted to spare you that, at least."

"So *when* were you going to tell me, then?" I asked suspiciously.

"This evening - but not like this," said Meg. "We didn't think about not walking past the cottage. We had no idea the new folk would have moved in so quickly," she went on.

There didn't seem to be much point in my going on about it. The deed was done, I couldn't alter it.

"It just seems so final," I said in a small voice. "I'll never be able to say goodbye to the cottage now - not properly." I wept inside for my little bedroom, for the sitting room with the welcoming open fire, for the kitchen, always so full of sunshine, where visitors always seemed to end up. I would never see it again.

The rest of my time in Cornwall went quickly – too quickly, I reflected. Maudie went back to school, and it felt really peculiar, not going back with her. I never thought I'd be sad at *not* going to school. Ben went back to Devon two days later. I felt so sad, saying goodbye to him. I wanted to tell him how much I'd miss him, but somehow I couldn't find the right words, so we ended up just saying a stiff little 'goodbye' on the morning he left. I knew I'd still be able to see him in the holidays – Meg and Charles had already invited me down for the summer ones – but it wouldn't be the same.

My last day was awful. I went round to say goodbye to Maudie and her parents after school. Maudie cried her eyes out and I felt like joining her. But I didn't: it suddenly seemed terribly important to pretend I didn't care about going. That way, it didn't hurt so much. Then I went to say goodbye to Ben's family and to Mrs Morris. Mrs Morris threw her arms round me and pressed me to her chest: I could hardly breathe. I was astonished – she never did things like that.

"Look after yourself, pet," she said. She surreptitiously wiped a tear from her eye. "And that father of yours – I shall miss you both."

Finally, I went up the cliff path with Rufus and a bag of stale bread. I wanted to say goodbye to the seagulls. They swooped and squawked as I threw the bread up to them.

"Goodbye," I breathed as I tossed the last crust up into the air. "Goodbye, seagulls – but it's not goodbye forever.

I'll be back – I promise you, I'll be back soon!"

And one day, I vowed, I'll be back for good.

I suddenly became aware that the car had stopped. My pretending to be asleep must, at some stage, have turned into reality because my eyes were closed and my head had slipped sideways against Fishpaste's basket.

"Lizzie!" Meg's voice drifted through my thoughts. "Lizzie, wake up – we're there! We've arrived!"

I opened one eye. My head and limbs hurt – I must have been asleep for a couple of hours.

I struggled to sit up. Then I noticed we were parked outside the house in Barnes – so it was true. We were really there. I wished I'd stayed asleep. At least I'd been having a pleasant dream.

Rufus was leaping around excitedly in the back. He wanted to get out and explore. He noticed I was awake and started to lick my face.

"Get off me, Rufus," I said crossly, pushing him away. I felt in a thoroughly bad mood.

Meg and Charles got out of the car and went to ring the doorbell. I toyed with the idea of getting out too and running away, but dismissed the thought. Where would I go? I had no money on me and I would have to leave the animals behind. I didn't have time to run away, anyway, because there, coming down the path arm in arm, silly sickly smiles on their faces, were Daddy and Miss Bullock. Daddy's mouth was moving like a goldfish's and I realised he was saying something to me. I couldn't hear what it was because the car window was closed. I should really have wound it down and said something warm and daughterly, but I didn't feel like it. I ignored him and stared sulkily out of the other window. Daddy opened the passenger door.

"Lizzie!" he said happily. "How are you, sweetie? Did you have a good trip?" He didn't even realise I'd purposely ignored him.

"No," I said, "it was horrible." I still sat there, staring out of the window. Rufus was going bananas behind me at the sight of Daddy.

"Shut up, Rufus," I said. "It's only Daddy."

"Come on then," Daddy said to me. "Let's get you all inside – and how's my smashing granddaughter then?" he said to Katey. Ridiculous – she couldn't understand what he was saying, she's far too young. But she held out her arms to him, all the same, and gurgled wetly.

I got out of the car and slammed the door, hard. *She* was standing there, waiting.

"Hello, Lizzie," she said. She kissed my cheek. I shrank back involuntarily, but nobody noticed.

"Say hello to Wendy, then," said Daddy, letting Rufus out of the car.

"Hello, Miss Bullock," I mumbled. For some reason, they thought this hilarious.

"You must start calling her Wendy," laughed Daddy. "She's not Miss Bullock any more, you know – she's Mrs Oliver now." They looked at each other sloppily and entwined fingers. I looked away and didn't answer. I could never call her Wendy: *never*. She'd always be Miss Bullock to me. As for being Mrs Oliver – there was only one Mrs Oliver; my mother. And she was dead. And here was my father now, laughing and holding hands with this woman, who was only a few years older than his elder daughter. I felt sick.

Just then, Meg came out. She noticed my pale face and hurried me indoors.

"I knew you'd feel like this," she said anxiously. "It's falling asleep in the car – you're always the same." She sat me down and gave me a drink of water. I began to feel a bit better and looked around. The house seemed in chaos. There were half-unpacked tea-chests everywhere and dust sheets thrown carelessly over the furniture. Everything seemed to be in the wrong room – the television was in the kitchen and I could see a new washing machine sitting squarely in the middle of the hallway. I suddenly felt very weary. I could barely keep my eyes open.

"Do you think I could have a lie-down somewhere?" I asked Meg. I could see Daddy bringing in Fishpaste's basket. Rufus was romping around in the back garden exploring the undergrowth. Meg nodded.

"Of course you can – though I think you'll have to use Daddy's room. None of the other beds have been made

up yet." She looked rather cross. "I did think they might have got things straightened out a *bit* in the time they've been here. Oh well," she went on distractedly, "Charles and I will have to set to, I suppose."

Meg showed me into the large front bedroom. I took my shoes off and lay down on the double bed on top of the duvet. I'd taken the cat basket up with me, and Fishpaste immediately jumped out on to the bed and started to clean himself furiously. He hadn't liked it in the car: he couldn't see where he was going, and it had upset him.

Then I noticed that the photograph of my mother, which Daddy usually kept by his bed, had gone. In its place was one of Miss Bullock in the long grey dress she'd worn on New Year's Eve; she was smiling shyly and showing off the diamond engagement ring Daddy had given her. I also noticed feminine things on the other bedside table: a pot of handcream, a romantic novel.

I carefully moved on to Daddy's side of the bed and laid Miss Bullock's photograph face-downwards on the table. I can't sleep with that looking at me, I told myself. Then I closed my eyes and slept until Meg came to wake me for supper.

2

Oaklands and Amber

I'd never realised it took so long to sort things out after moving house. Life would be so much easier if you could just move the whole building, with the furniture and stuff still inside. Just lift the house up with a crane or something, and plonk it down in the new spot – wouldn't that look funny!

Meg and Charles spent the whole weekend helping: moving furniture from room to room, scrubbing walls and floors, unpacking tea-chests and crates. Daddy was a bit worried about Meg – her baby was due in about three months and he kept telling her to go and sit down. She wouldn't, though – she kept tutting, and washing crockery and ornaments.

She and Charles stayed the whole weekend – and it's just as well they did. I hate to think how long it would have taken Daddy and Miss Bullock if they'd been on their own. They kept standing in corners, gazing stupidly into each other's eyes without saying anything. I don't know what they were playing at: it looked ridiculous.

Rufus settled down quite quickly – he loved the overgrown garden and, anyway, he's always quite happy as long as he's got his people and his blanket. It's smelly, but it means 'home' to him, wherever it's put down.

But Fishpaste hated it. He hid under my bed and wouldn't come out, except at night when he jumped on to my tummy as usual. I had to give him a litter tray and feed him on saucers which I pushed under the bed. He hadn't purred for ages. I knew exactly how he felt, because my feelings were the same. I wished I had a blanket like Rufus, which I could put down on to unfamiliar things to make them acceptable.

The room they had given me for a bedroom was huge and almost empty. It was an odd shape and had a large window with a padded window seat. That window seat was the best thing about the room. I could sit on it, and look right across the Common, and pretend I was in the country. All the room had in it was my bed and dressing table – they looked lost in the vast expanse. I didn't even have a carpet, or curtains, and there was a bare bulb hanging from the ceiling from about a metre of flex. The room wasn't cold, but felt it – cold and unfriendly. Yuck.

Hanging in the built-in wardrobes, amongst those clothes which I had got around to unpacking, was my new school uniform. I'd never seen such a lot of uniform before – games clothes, and PE clothes, and an apron for cookery lessons, and winter and summer uniform. It was all maroon and white – maroon pleated skirt, white blouse, maroon-and-white striped tie, maroon V-necked sweater. Maroon blazer trimmed with white braid, white and gold school badge on its pocket. Long white socks and maroon shoes. That was the winter uniform.

But I would be wearing the summer uniform when I started: a shapeless cotton dress in a sort of dark pink-and-white check, with a stretchy belt (the sort nurses wear) round the middle. I could wear the blazer on top, or a maroon gabardine mackintosh. I'd gone right off maroon – I used to like it, too. I'd never seen so much of it in one place at once.

My new school was apparently very 'select'; it was private, and all girls, about five miles away. ('Select' was *Her* description of it. I bet I know who selected it, too.) I would go there on the school bus which stopped at the top of our road. How amazingly convenient, I thought sourly. I could just envisage the school bus now – maroon, I bet, full of maroon morons.

I started there on the day Meg, Charles and Katey were going back to Cornwall. I would have given anything to have been able to go with them. Instead, here I was, dressed in that stupid pink-and-white dress, trying not to feel sick with nervousness at the thought of the day ahead.

After breakfast, I went upstairs to say goodbye to them. Meg and Charles were sitting up in bed, drinking cups of tea, and Katey was tucked up in between them. She chuckled when she saw me, and clambered over the bed to the end, holding her arms out to be picked up.

I obliged. She kissed my cheek wetly and I could smell her lovely clean, baby-powder smell. She was getting bigger by the day – she was over a year old now and nearly too heavy for me to hold.

"Bye bye, Katey," I said to her. "Just you wait until you go to school – you'll understand what I'm going through then."

"What bliss!" sighed Meg. "I can't wait until she starts – and the other one, too." She patted the Bump.

"I thought you liked them – babies, I mean," I said, putting Katey back down on the bed.

"I do," answered Meg, "but it'll be lovely to have some time to myself again – watch out, Charles!" Katey had decided to investigate her Daddy's teacup and was making a grab for it.

"See what I mean?" said Meg, laughing.

"Bye, Lizzie," said Charles, putting his cup safely down. "Mind you settle down soon, now - we'll be thinking about you." He gave me a kiss.

"You are coming to us for the holidays, aren't you?" asked Meg.

"I think so - part of them, anyway. Daddy says we've got to spend some time with *Her* parents - Miss Bullock's, I mean," I amended hastily.

"Well, just let us know how long you want to stay, and you'll be very welcome," Meg said. She didn't seem to notice I'd said 'Miss Bullock'. She hugged me tightly. "Bye now, Lizzie - take care of yourself."

Tears pricked my eyelids. I didn't want them to go - they were my last remaining link with Cornwall. But go they must.

I went downstairs with my school bag, empty of books, and shouted goodbye to Daddy and Miss Bullock. He had wanted to accompany me to the school today, my first day, but I'd told him not to.

"I don't want you holding my hand, Daddy - I can manage," I'd said. "Anyway, they'll all think I'm a terrible baby if you do." I think Daddy was a bit taken aback, but he'd agreed.

I must admit to feeling a bit lonely, though, as I trudged out to catch the school bus.

That ride to school on the bus immediately removed all my previous ideas about boys being the rowdy ones. There were only about twenty-five girls on the bus, but the noise was like the monkey house at the zoo. Bags were thrown around, books flying everywhere. Girls scrambled over the seats, looking very undignified. Some of them were making rude gestures out of the back window at the drivers on the road behind us.

As I didn't know anybody, I felt quite tongue-tied with shyness. I stared out of the window, trying to ignore the racket around me. I got bored watching the traffic after a while so I started to watch the girls in the bus. It looked as if one girl in particular was the sort of ring-leader. She was the only one, apart from me, actually sitting in a seat, but she was egging everybody else on. She had a very posh voice, but her language was awful – full of swear words. (What Mrs Morris would call 'dirty talk'.) I could only see the back of her head, but she looked as though she was pretty – her hair was long and very blonde. At last, the bus swung through a set of iron gates with a sign saying 'Oaklands'. As I got off the bus, I noticed the blonde girl, surrounded by about four others, standing looking at me. Then she came over.

She was half a head taller than me and she was very pretty. Her skin was like porcelain, her eyes very blue and, although she was wearing the same dress as the rest of us, it somehow looked different on her. I guessed she was about fifteen.

I smiled at her, thinking she was waiting to show me to the school. I was wrong.

"New girl," she said imperiously. "What's your name?" Her voice really was very posh.

"Lizzie," I said. My smile had faded a bit.

"I meant your surname, creep."

My smile disappeared completely.

"My name's Lizzie Oliver," I said. "What's yours?" Her hangers-on giggled.

"Moi name's Lizzie Oliver," they mimicked.

"Ooh-aar – ooh-aar!" said the blonde one.

I realised they were trying to imitate my accent, which I suppose is Cornish. Their accents sounded pretty daft to me, as well, but I wasn't taking the mickey out of *them*.

"What's *your* name?" I asked the blonde girl again. The others fell about in helpless laughter.

"Ooh-aar – ooh-aar!" they mocked.

"Ooh-aar Oliver!" said the blonde one. "Perfect! – that's what we'll call you!" They all walked off in fits of giggles. "Ooh-aar!" I heard them shout.

"My name's Lizzie! *Lizzie!*" I shouted after them. But they'd gone. I trudged after them, up the drive, and found myself in front of a large house. There was a bell set into the wall beside the front door, so I pressed it. Nothing happened. I tried the door knob – it turned, so I opened the door and went in. I was in a large, panelled entrance hall, with doors leading off it. As I was trying to decide where to go next, one of the doors opened and a middle-aged lady with a bun stepped into the hall. Her face went stern when she saw me.

"You – little gel!" she said frostily. That put me off for a start: I loathe and detest being called "little girl". "What are you doing?" she went on. "You know Juniors aren't allowed in here."

To my annoyance, I went red and started to mumble. "Well – actually ..." I stammered.

"Well nothing," she said crisply. "It's quite against school rules. Come along – off you go!" She made shooing gestures with her hands, as though I were a chicken.

I stood my ground. "Well, actually," I started again, "I'm new – a new pupil, I mean. I've got to see the Headmistress."

Her face thawed about half a degree.

"Why on earth didn't you say so before?" I didn't think it wise to point out she'd hardly given me the chance.

"Come along," she said, "I'd better take you to her."

She whisked me to a door with 'Miss Carrington-Smythe' written on it. She knocked twice, then went off and left me there. For one brief moment I had a strong urge to run away, out of the massive front door, away from this horrible school. Because I knew for sure that it *was* a horrible school. But I didn't have time to do anything of the kind.

"Enter!" boomed a voice from inside. I opened the door, knees knocking, and went in.

Miss Carrington-Smythe was a large, loud lady. She was very smartly dressed and reminded me of a younger version of Mrs Bullock. She spoke rather like her, too – as though she had something in her mouth. When she spoke, just her lips moved – nothing else. It made her look unreal, like a puppet. She gave me my timetable and told me my form teacher's name was Miss Jenkins.

"Jennifer will show you to your form room," she said. "She is our Head Prefect. If you need any assistance in finding classrooms, just ask anyone. All our gels are very helpful."

I hoped the blonde one I'd met earlier wasn't an example of this helpfulness.

"Thank you," I said and stood up to go.

"Just one moment – aah – Elizabeth," she said. "I was expecting your father to accompany you today. May I enquire why you are here on your own?"

"I didn't want him to come," I replied. "I wanted to manage on my own."

"Indeed?" She regarded me over the top of her half-spectacles. "And do you always get what you want?"

"Not always, no," I said honestly. "It's just that ..."

"Never mind, never mind." She waved an impatient hand at me. "We do not encourage wilful behaviour here at Oaklands. We pride ourselves on team spirit – pulling together – that sort of thing. I feel you would do well to bear that in mind." I said nothing. I stared at the cut glass ink bottle on Miss Carrington-Smythe's desk. Silly old bag, I thought.

"And while I am on that subject," she went on, consulting a piece of paper on her desk, "I gather you play the – aah – piano?" She pronounced it "pee-arno".

"Violin," I corrected her.

"Quite, quite." She studied the paper. "And I see you were given permission to miss games lessons at your previous school."

"That's right," I agreed, "I used to do extra music ..."

"Elizabeth," she interrupted, "when I require additional information from you, I shall ask for it. In the meantime, all I require is a simple 'yes' or 'no'. Do you understand?"

"Yes, but ..."

"A simple 'yes' or 'no'," she repeated sternly. "Which is it to be?"

"I – I can't remember the question," I said lamely. She put the paper down sharply and looked hard at me.

"Are you being insolent, gel?" she boomed.

"No – no!" That was two noes. If I wasn't careful, she'd tell me off for that, too.

"You were allowed to miss games lessons at your previous school – is that right?" She wasn't convinced about the insolence, I could see that.

"Yes."

"Well, let me assure you, you won't be missing them here. We are very keen on sport here at Oaklands. We finished last season with the best hockey results in the area, and our tennis captain has been picked to represent England in the Under-18 team." She puffed up with pride like a thrush.

"How wonderful," I said dutifully. How boring, I thought. I hate tennis.

"We think so," she preened. "We take games very seriously here at Oaklands." I was getting sick of that phrase, 'here at Oaklands'. "Teaches one team spirit. So I'm afraid you won't be bunking off games here. Now then," she said, reaching for her telephone, "I think that's all. I'll just get Jennifer to show you to your class." She spoke briskly down the telephone and replaced the receiver with a bang.

Jennifer was a pudding-like lump of a girl with very bad skin. She wordlessly showed me to a classroom, then turned and vanished like a phantom.

I took a deep breath, turned the handle and went in. Twenty-five heads turned in my direction, twenty-five pairs of eyes stared at me. I blushed at all the attention. Then I noticed a kind-looking lady sitting at the teacher's desk at the far end of the room. I swallowed hard.

"Miss Jenkins?" I asked.

"Yes," she agreed. She smiled at me. "Who are you?" I felt encouraged – it was the first friendly face I'd seen since arriving at the horrid place.

"I'm Lizzie Oliver," I said. "I'm new," I added by way of explanation. "I'm in your class." Somebody snorted, then giggled.

"Be quiet, Amber," said Miss Jenkins sternly. "Come in," she said to me. "Come in and shut the door. I'm just calling the register. You can sit there – next to Amber. Amber Delaney – move over, let Elizabeth sit down."

Amber Delaney – what a beautiful name, I thought. I rolled it, smooth, over my tongue. Then I realised the owner of this enchanting name was none other than the blonde girl from the bus. She looked at me slyly.

"She can't sit here, Miss," she said in that posh voice of hers. "I'm saving it for Camilla. She's at the dentist this morning – I promised I'd save her a seat." She narrowed her eyes and regarded me unwaveringly.

Miss Jenkins sighed. "Oh, very well then – you'd better sit here, Elizabeth – here, at the front."

My neighbour was a dark, sullen-looking girl called Harriet who didn't say a word to me all morning. I felt very much alone, and not at all impressed with my new school.

As I sat eating my solitary lunch, I went through the morning's events in my mind. I was already finding it hard to understand what was happening in the lessons, but I told myself part of that was starting a new school, part-way through the term. It was bound to be strange at first.

Amber Delaney had approached me during break, accompanied by her hangers-on and the girl Camilla, back from the dentist. I was suddenly reminded of Neil Trewin and his gang at my old school, taunting Maudie on her first day. Only I was playing the part of Maudie now, and there was nobody to take my rôle: to stick up for me, to tell them to get lost. I gritted my teeth and turned away. I will not cry, I told myself, I will not cry, as the taunts of "Ooh-aar! Ooh-aar!" filled my ears.

"Ooh-aar Oliver!" sneered Amber. "What's the matter – can't you speak English?" She poked me in the ribs. All at once, I'd had enough of her.

"Why are you picking on me?" I said. I should have kept my mouth shut. At the sound of my voice they burst into paroxysms of laughter.

"Oh – oh!" laughed Amber weakly. "Her voice! It's too funny – oh, I can't bear it!" She clutched her sides.

I looked at her. She really was very pretty. I couldn't believe she was only thirteen, the same as me. She was wearing make-up, and mingled with the smell of her scent was another smell, a grown-up one – then I realised what it was. Cigarettes! Surely she didn't smoke? Why, she was much too young! She was still laughing, in a very affected way. I had to stop her. I couldn't stand her awful cackling any longer.

"You're a silly cow," I informed her.

Her laughter stopped as though a tap had been turned off. She stepped closer to me and pushed her face near to mine.

"*What* did you call me?" she demanded.

"You heard," I replied. I wasn't feeling as brave as I sounded. She was bigger than me, and she had all her gang with her.

"I don't think I did," she said, an odd note in her voice. So I repeated it for her.

"You – are – a – silly – cow." There was no mistaking it this time.

For a moment, we just stood and looked at each other, like two cats on a wall. Then, very slowly, very deliberately, she lifted her hand – and slapped my face, hard.

I was stunned. I stood there, blood singing in my ears, not knowing what she would do next.

She spoke, very quietly – I could hear the fury in her voice. "Nobody," she said, "nobody – ever – calls me that – and gets away with it." Then she turned on her heel and walked off, her cohorts scattering after her, giggling and whispering.

I finished my pudding and pushed the plate away. As I sat there, I considered the situation. Amber seemed determined to make my life at Oaklands a misery. Well, I wasn't going to let her. The way I saw it, Amber Delaney and I were at war.

3

Pippa befriends me

The first weeks at Oaklands were sheer misery. Nobody wanted to be my friend, and I didn't know why not. I suspected it had something to do with Amber Delaney, but I couldn't understand why she should have so much influence on everybody else. I wasn't used to being deliberately ignored. I hated it – at my old school I'd always had plenty of friends. I didn't know what to do to get people to like me. I'd never had to do it before: they'd always seemed to like me naturally. I ached for Ben and Maudie. Things were made worse by the unfamiliar surroundings. The house at Barnes was at last in some kind of order, but I didn't know the area, didn't know where I could go for one of my walks with Rufus. The Common was always full of courting couples and people walking their dogs – not exactly the place for a quiet think, but it had to do.

One afternoon, after school, I saw a likely-looking clump of bushes on the Common and made for it, thinking I could sit amongst them, alone, and ruminate. But when I got there, I nearly fell over a boy and girl lying on the ground, snogging. I was so embarrassed – I just stood there for a moment. Then I realised Rufus would probably come crashing in at any second, so I sort of murmured "sorry" and backed off. I don't think they even noticed – they just carried on, as though they were stuck together at the mouth. I wonder what that sort of kissing is like – I wonder how you breathe?

Anyway, as I was saying, it was awfully difficult to get any privacy to think of a plan of action against Amber Delaney. It was no good sitting in my room: Daddy or Miss Bullock kept calling me to give them a hand with this, that or the other. I knew they were trying to keep me occupied. I overheard her saying to Daddy: "We mustn't let Lizzie sit in her room, brooding." It made me sound like a chicken. I'd have been quite happy left to brood.

Another thing was, Miss Bullock kept coming into my room to have nice, girly little chats – at least, that's what she wanted. She didn't get them though – for one thing, I didn't feel I had anything to say to her, and for another, the things she wanted to talk about were – well, embarrassing. One day, she was sorting through my school blouses when she suddenly came out with: "I think it's about time we bought you a bra"!! I ask you! I just went red.

On another occasion she knocked on the door and came in. Then she stood there, fiddling with the ornaments on my dressing table. After about five minutes of this I said: "What was it you wanted? – only I've got homework to do." I couldn't stand her fiddling around any longer.

She said: "I wanted to talk to you about babies." I was mystified.

"Babies?" I repeated.

"Well," she went on, not looking at me, "not babies exactly – more, well, where they come from."

I breathed a sigh of relief. For a moment, I thought she was going to tell me she was going to have one.

"Oh, that's all right," I said nonchalantly, "I already know about all that. We learned about it at school."

"Yes, but ..." she said. She wanted to talk about it, I could tell, but I got all my homework books out, so she had to go away. I wasn't going to discuss the Facts of Life with *her*; I didn't even talk about that sort of thing with Meg.

Of course, all this embarrassing sort of talk happened quite a bit later on, when we'd all been at Barnes for several weeks. For the first couple of weeks – my worst time at school – she and Daddy were talking to me about finding me a violin teacher, and how was I getting on at school. I just said "OK" to that – I didn't want them to know nobody talked to me. They might think it was my fault. I was finding the lessons hard, too. I knew I'd been put in the wrong set – everybody else was much cleverer than me – but when I mentioned it, nervously, to Miss Jenkins she just said, "Nonsense! You'll soon settle down, once you get used to our way of doing things." But I knew I'd never get used to their way of doing things.

All in all, I was thoroughly miserable. Amber Delaney's campaign to get at me was in full swing and my own plan of retaliation hadn't even been thought out yet.

Amber was still mocking my voice whenever she got the chance. Not only did she make fun of my normal speaking voice, but she seemed to think my accent when I spoke French was the funniest thing she'd heard. That annoyed me; I knew I was good at French, much better than she was. She spoke French exactly the same way she spoke English, complete with drawling upper-class accent.

Apart from the mocking, things kept going missing from my bag when I knew I'd put them there that morning. My history homework disappeared, only to reappear, torn in half, long after the lesson (when I'd been thoroughly told off). One cookery lesson, when we were supposed to be making rock cakes, the ingredients I'd brought from home were replaced by those for shepherd's pie which we'd made the previous week.

When we were all getting changed for PE one morning, I couldn't find my maroon PE knickers. I knew I'd packed them – I'd taken them from the airing cupboard myself that morning. The PE teacher made me do the lesson anyway, in my ordinary white ones. It was awful. When I told her I couldn't find the maroon ones, she fixed me with a stern eye and said, "It won't wash, Elizabeth Oliver. I've heard all the excuses going for missing PE, that one included. Get changed."

When I protested feebly, she looked even crosser and said; "I've heard all about you and your famous memory – or lack of it. Get changed." She was like a parrot – she seemed to end every sentence with "Get changed". But it was true – I was getting a reputation for forgetting things, which wasn't fair. I didn't forget them – Amber and her colleagues were hiding them.

PE and games were the bane of my life. Oaklands took sporty things very seriously indeed, as the Head warned me on my first day. I hated them. I couldn't see the fun of throwing myself over wooden horses, and standing around on a freezing cold hockey pitch in the middle of winter seemed the height of lunacy to me. Tennis I couldn't bear – my racquet always seemed to have a huge, invisible hole in it, allowing the ball to go straight through – and as for the rounders: well! Nobody ever wanted me on their side for rounders. I can't say I blamed them. I'm frightened of the ball for one thing; it isn't much use if you close your eyes when you're supposed to be catching the wretched thing.

Our games lessons were a double period before lunch on Fridays – the only good thing about that was I had a whole weekend to recover. There was a boys' school near Oaklands which broke for lunch earlier than us, and all the boys would come over and congregate round the tennis courts, whistling and shouting. Amber Delaney and her crowd would hit their tennis balls purposely over in the boys' direction, and then spend ages retrieving them – bending over and showing lots of leg. Mrs Fotherington, the games mistress ('mistress' – I ask you! A typical Oaklands word) would flap around like an old mother hen, trying vainly to round them up.

"Gels, gels!" she would twitter. "Come over here and let me show you the top-spin forehand volley!" But Amber Delaney was much more interested in the boys than in Mrs Fotherington's top-spin forehand volley – anyone could see that.

There were lots of rumours flying around about Amber Delaney and boys – even I, whom nobody talked to, got to hear of them. Somebody had written "Amber Delaney DOES IT with Craig Johnstone" on one of the lavatory walls. I wasn't exactly sure what IT was that Amber Delaney was supposed to do – but I knew it was something rude.

Whatever Amber did was rude, or naughty, in one way or another. It never ceased to amaze me, the difference between her beautiful, angelic face, and the way she behaved. The way she spoke, too: awful swear words coming from those beautiful lips in that posh accent of hers. She never misbehaved in lessons, though – or not when the teachers were around, at any rate. She was far too cunning for that. All the teachers thought she was wonderful – and clever, too. That's because she always got the clever girls in the class to do her homework for her, on pain of having some foul deed done to them if they didn't comply.

I loathed her: but she fascinated me, too. I watched her for hours, telling myself I had to find out her weakness in order to get my own back. I knew she must have a weakness – everybody does – but in the end I didn't have to discover it. She showed me it herself.

When the music teacher, Miss Berkowitz, found out about me – my violin-playing, I mean – she got me to play in the school orchestra. She was rather nice, in a brusque sort of way. "Madam doesn't consider music 'quate naice' as a career for her gels," she told me once. ('Madam' was Miss Carrington-Smythe.) "I'm up against it all the time. But *you'll* find it worse," she said. "You've got the spark – talent. You'll have to look outside this school to develop it – you'll stifle here."

I'd been at Oaklands about three weeks when Miss Berkowitz asked me to stay after school, so she could hear my playing before I joined the school orchestra. When I finished, she nodded, and laughed drily.

"If you'll have us," she said, "we'll have you." Just then, there was a knock on the music-room door and a girl with short red hair came in. She reminded me a bit of Maudie.

"Oh, Pippa," said Miss Berkowitz to her. "Good. This is Lizzie Oliver – she's a violinist." The girl smiled at me.

"Hello," she said. "I'm Pippa Burns."

I was dazed – a smile, *and* being called Lizzie. I'd been Elizabeth since I'd started at Oaklands, to my disgust. Miss Berkowitz went on.

"Pippa's in the fifth form," she told me, "doing her exams this term."

"Oh," I said. I didn't see what that had to do with me.

"I'm going to music college when I'm seventeen," said Pippa, still smiling at me. Lucky you, I thought, getting away from this dump.

"She's an accompanist," said Miss Berkowitz to me. "I thought it would be good for both of you to do some practice together." Pippa looked a bit doubtful. She was obviously wondering what she was being let in for.

"What grade are you?" she asked me. (She meant the Associated Board music exams, of course.)

"It's OK," I assured her. "I did Grade 8 last year, but I haven't had any lessons for a while. Daddy's trying to find me a teacher," I said. I wished he'd get around to it. Pippa was reassured and we arranged to do some practice the following day.

She came home with me after school: as we walked to the bus together, several fifth-formers said goodbye to her and smiled at me. I was reminded vividly of Maudie's experiences at my old school. I could now understand her gratitude for my friendship, the gratitude which I'd dismissed at the time as 'drippy'.

When we got home Miss Bullock was there, waiting. "Hello, Lizzie," she greeted me. "Oh, how nice – you've brought a friend home!"

"Who's that?" asked Pippa, when we were in the room with the piano – "the Music Room", Daddy called it, rather grandly I thought.

"That's Miss Bullock," I said.

"Is she the *au pair*?"

"No, she's ..." I didn't want to use the word 'stepmother'. "She's married to my father."

"Oh, your stepmother." Pippa had no such qualms. She frowned suddenly. "Hang on – if she's married to your father, why's she called Miss Bullock?"

"Well – I s'pose she's not really, not any more. But that's what I've always called her."

"And you can't get used to calling her anything else?"

"No." That was it, exactly – I was grateful Pippa understood. But that doesn't explain what made me say what I told her next.

"My real mother's dead," I said, mustering a sob in my voice. "She died when I was ten – in a car crash. It was awful." I think I was trying to get her sympathy – I felt quite ashamed of myself. But I was taken aback at her response.

"Oh," she said casually. "My parents are divorced. I wish *my* mother was dead – I have to live with her. I'd much rather live with my father – he understands me." I was shocked – fancy wishing your parents dead!

"How dreadful for them – being divorced, I mean," I said quietly. Pippa laughed.

"You wouldn't say that if you knew them – can't stand the sight of each other. My mother's a cow: I can understand how father feels." She sounded cheerful enough about it, anyway. I tried again.

"But – isn't it rather odd?"

"Odd? No, of course not. Half the girls at school have parents who are divorced or separated. It's normal these days."

Not in Cornwall, I thought. I'd never get used to London.

Over tea, we talked about music. Pippa raised the subject of Amber Delaney when Miss Bullock had gone to wash the tea things.

"That Delaney brat is a real nuisance," she declared. "I can't understand the hold she has, myself – tried it on me, once, but I just told her to run away and play. She never did it again."

"But you're older than me," I said, "and bigger. And you're in different classes. She gets at me by hiding my things and getting her friends to join in."

"Does it really bother you?"

"Well – I try not to let it. But it's horrid, being ignored and everything."

"Look, don't worry," said Pippa. "One of my friends has a sister who's one of Amber's hangers-on. Harriet Smith – d'you know her?"

I remembered the girl I'd been sat next to on my first day, and nodded. "But *she* can't do anything – I'm sure Amber doesn't take any notice of what she says."

"Leave it with me – I'll have a word with her. I don't think you'll be ignored too much any more – not by everyone, at any rate."

I never knew what Pippa said, or even why anything she may have said should have any effect. But it did seem to. The next day, Harriet asked to borrow my ruler. Then, two of her friends spoke to me during the morning break.

After that, people seemed to forget they were supposed to be ignoring me. Nobody was what you might call over-friendly, but at least they were talking to me. All except Amber and her hard core of Mafioso, that is – they would still pass me on the stairs and stick out a foot to trip me up, amid cries of "Ooh-aar! Ooh-aar!" But I found it much easier to ignore them now.

Then one day, during a games lesson actually, Amber unwittingly provided me with the ammunition to fire at her. One of the girls stopped the rounders ball in a rather spectacular fashion, with her nose, which immediately started to gush blood. She clutched at her nose with one hand, and the nearest girl with the other.

The nearest girl happened to be Amber. She took one look at the blood, uttered a funny little cry, turned pale green and fell on the ground. The rest of us watched the little drama with interest; then Mrs Fotherington came charging in in her usual haphazard way and started taking control. The girl with the nosebleed was despatched to the medical room, leaning heavily on Harriet's shoulders. Mrs Fotherington bent down to where Amber lay, blonde hair trailing in the mud.

"Come on, dear," she said, sticking a phial of smelling salts under Amber's nose.

"Uughgh," said Amber, eyelids flickering.

"It's the blood, you see," Camilla was informing anyone who cared to listen. "Poor Amber – she's always been terrified of blood. She's got such a sensitive soul."

Sensitive my left elbow, I thought. She's about as sensitive as a praying mantis. But she had given me the answer to my little problem: I would sicken Amber Delaney into submission.

4

The Liver Incident

When I packed my school bag on Monday morning, I carefully included a gunky-looking paper package wrapped tightly in several plastic bags. The plastic was to stop the blood oozing through the paper onto my books: for what it contained was one pound of finely chopped, best quality, raw ... *liver*! I'd taken it from the freezer over the weekend. It was intended for Rufus and Fishpaste - they love liver - but I knew they wouldn't mind me having it. I explained to them that it was going to be put to good use.

I'd thought my plan through carefully. We had a period of PE immediately after break on Monday mornings, followed by one of French which took us up to lunchtime. Amber always brought a packed lunch to school in a little plastic box, and she had a habit of dipping into her lunchbox during the last lesson before lunch and coming up with bits of sandwich which she would then furtively eat. I'd seen her doing it: she would put her bag on the floor under her desk and surreptitiously rummage through it with one hand, always keeping her eyes on the teacher. She'd been told off for eating in class several times, but it didn't stop her – she was just greedy.

If I could make some excuse to slip out of the PE class, I could substitute the sandwiches in her lunchbox for a nice, tasty little snack of my own recipe – the raw liver ...

I hugged my secret to myself as I sat on the school bus. I couldn't wait to see Amber's face when her greedy fingers found the surprise treat in her lunchbox!

I managed to leave the gymnasium while the lesson was in progress without too much trouble. I pretended I needed my hanky, which I'd purposely left in my coat pocket in the changing room.

"Go and fetch it, then," said the PE teacher with a sigh. "And hurry up about it!"

I worked quickly when I got into the changing room. I found Amber's bag and emptied the sandwiches into the rubbish bin. Then I tipped the liver into the lunchbox, snapped the lid back on, and put the yukky plastic bags into the bin with the sandwiches, covering the whole lot with scrunched-up paper towels to hide the evidence. I put the lunchbox back into Amber's bag, got my hanky, and went back into the gym – the whole exercise had only taken about two minutes.

I didn't have long to wait to witness the results of my handiwork. Soon after we all filed into the classroom for the next lesson, Amber had her bag on the floor and was rummaging around in it. The French teacher droned on: "Now repeat after me: *Je vais, tu vas, il va, elle va.*" We obediently repeated the verb. Amber's fingers dug around in her bag. I could hardly bear to watch.

"... *nous allons, vous allez – alors,* Ambaire Delaney, what are you doing?"

I caught my breath. The teacher had noticed Amber's wandering attention. Would everything be spoilt?

"Nothing, Madame." Amber's reply was sweetly innocent. She sat up straight.

"Then kindly geev me the benefeet of your entire attention."

"*Oui*, Madame." Amber's accent was perfect for once. Madame, satisfied, turned her back to the class and began to write the Imperfect Tense of '*Aller*' on the blackboard. Amber resumed her quest for food in her bag. I watched her, fascinated and terrified at the same time.

It was worth waiting for. As her fingers found the horrid, squelchy, mushy mess in the lunchbox, Amber's face registered surprise, incomprehension, horror and shock, all at once. She gave a gasp and tried to pull her hand away: but her fingers must have been caught under the snap-lid because she lifted the whole thing clear of her bag. She stared at the blue box dangling at the end of her wrist, looking for all the world like some outlandish lobster holding her hand in its claws.

Amber gibbered and shook her wrist, hard. The top of the lunchbox snapped off, releasing her hand, but sending bloody chopped liver everywhere. A couple of girls recoiled in horror, but most were watching the scene with interest.

Amber noticed the blood from the meat, which was staining her hand to the wrist, and she started to scream. She just opened her mouth and out came this awful noise. She wouldn't stop.

Several of the girls started to titter. Madame rushed over from the blackboard to try and stop the dreadful racket.

"Be quiet, Ambaire!" she said. "Whatever ees the

matter? You're not 'urt, are you? Shut thees noise up!"

The class, taking advantage of this unusual diversion, were creased up with laughter at the sight of the wild-eyed girl, surrounded by liver, screaming her head off. Even Camilla, Amber's great friend, was helpless with mirth.

Madame took Amber by the shoulders and shook her vigorously. Amber's head whipped back and forth with the movement. She stopped screaming and broke instead into noisy sobs.

"That's bettair," said Madame. "She ought to go and lie down – 'oo will take 'er to the Medical Room?"

I volunteered immediately: I wanted Amber to know who was responsible for the liver. Outside the Medical Room, I looked at her face. It was red and blotchy with tears: she looked very different from her normal, self-assured self. I hissed into her ear.

"*I* put the liver there," I whispered, "but if you tell anyone I'll deny it."

She sniffed loudly and regarded me with hatred.

"There's more where that came from," I went on. "so if you don't leave me alone, you'd better watch out!"

And with that warning, I knocked on the door and took her, still sniffing, in to Matron.

Things seemed to change slightly at school following the Liver Incident, as I called it. I'm sure Amber hadn't spread the word around wholly by herself – it would have meant such a loss of face – but people still seemed to have heard about it. Girls would grin at me in the corridor instead of turning away from me. Pippa said, "Well done, kid," in an undertone when I passed her on the stairs the day after the Incident. Only Amber and Camilla continued to ignore me – although their spiteful taunts seemed to have stopped, temporarily at least.

I still wasn't happy at Oaklands: I felt altogether too much like a fish out of water for that. But it was, at least, more bearable. Towards the end of the Liver week, Harriet surprised me by asking if I wanted to go to the Youth Club disco on Friday evening.

"Wh – when?" I said, taken aback. "Where?"

"Half past seven – the Youth Club's on Putney Hill."

"I don't know," I said. I'd never been to a disco before – they weren't much in demand in Penwithin.

"Oh, well," said Harriet, shrugging and turning away. "If you're not interested ..."

"Oh, I am, I am," I said hurriedly. I wanted to go – to make friends, to talk to people. "Thanks for asking me, Harriet."

"OK," she replied. "I'll wait for you outside, shall I? Say, twenty past. Oh, by the way," she added as an afterthought, "it costs a pound."

That posed a problem. I'd long since spent all my pocket money for the week, on a new violin string, and I wasn't due for any more until Sunday. *That* money was earmarked for some sheet music I needed. I dismissed the problem: I'd get the money somehow.

To my surprise, Daddy agreed I could go to the disco.

"I'll drive you there," he said, "and I'll come to collect you. I'll be outside at half past nine, sharp."

That seemed ridiculously early to me. "But, Daddy," I began to protest.

"Sharp," he repeated firmly. "You're still only thirteen – I don't know anybody who's going to be there, and there's some funny folk around." I knew better than to argue with him when he started going on about "funny folk". I was glad he was letting me go at all.

I took the money from Miss Bullock's purse – it was lying there, open, in her bag on top of the fridge. It was so easy just to remove a pound coin. I felt horribly guilty afterwards – I'd never done anything like that before – but I told myself she could well afford it. The purse was stuffed with coins and notes – she'll never even miss it, I told my pricking conscience.

Harriet was duly waiting for me outside the Youth Club. I was a bit late.

"Bye, Daddy," I said as I got out of the car. I waved as he drove off.

"Do you still call your father 'Daddy'?" asked Harriet scornfully.

"Yes – why, what's wrong?" I was puzzled.

"It's babyish," she scoffed. "I call mine 'Father' – have done for ages. Well, since last year, actually," she amended rather sheepishly.

"Oh," I said. I resolved to try and remember to call Daddy 'Father' from now on. Harriet was right – 'Daddy' *was* babyish. She was terribly sophisticated.

As we went into the Youth Club, the blaring music hit us with an almost physical force. The room was full of gyrating bodies and flashing lights – it seemed odd, as it was still quite light outside. I was suddenly gripped with nervousness. I didn't want to go in. It was too noisy, too hot and crowded.

"Go on, then," said Harriet, giving me a shove from behind. I had no choice. I paid my pound to the spotty boy on the door and we went in.

When my eyes got used to the gloom and the flashing lights, I started recognising people from school. Harriet brought me over a soggy paper cup of orange squash. I drank it and then we jiggled around half-heartedly to the thumping music. I felt very self-conscious: I didn't know what to do with my arms and legs. Everybody else was miles better at dancing than I was.

After about half an hour of this, I suddenly noticed a familiar blonde figure in the corner. It was Amber, but she was barely recognisable. She was clad in shiny black trousers that made her legs look like sticks of liquorice. The trousers were so tight, she looked as though she'd been poured into them and left to set. On the top she was wearing a frilly, white off-the-shoulder blouse which was very low-cut – if she'd had any front you'd have been able to see it. She had lots of make-up on and she held a cigarette between her scarlet painted fingers. On her feet she wore black sandals with four-inch heels, and her pale blonde hair was arranged in careful disarray on top of her head. The whole effect made her look about seventeen, and unbelievably trashy.

Just then, two things happened at once: the music changed to a slow record, and Amber noticed me. A boy of about sixteen detached himself from the crowd and led Amber in a bored fashion onto the dance floor. She entwined her arms round his neck and fixed me with her cool, unblinking stare.

I couldn't tear my eyes away. She was pressing herself against the boy – I wondered idly if he was the famous Craig Johnstone – and she never took her eyes off me during the whole dance. It felt as though she was mocking me, in some way I didn't understand.

When the dance was finished, she sauntered slowly towards me, a sneering smile on her lips. She stood in front of me on her high heels, legs apart, and put a fresh cigarette between her lips. She lit it and threw the spent match down at my feet. It was a sort of challenge, I knew. I felt frightened – I didn't know what to expect her to do next – and very childish, dressed as I was in my unremarkable skirt and blouse and stupid long white socks.

She blew a cloud of smoke into my face. I coughed.

"I haven't finished with you yet, Oliver," she said, "so you'd better just watch your step - understand?" Then she lifted her hand.

I thought she was going to hit me again. I didn't wait this time: I just turned and fled.

I was halfway up the road before I realised I was lost. I didn't have a clue where I was, or how to get home. Daddy was supposed to be meeting me at half past nine - it was now barely eight thirty. I could hardly roam around the unfamiliar streets of Putney for an hour. I decided I'd better find a phone box and ring for Daddy to come and fetch me.

First, find your phone box, I thought to myself. I found one, but it was out of order. The street it was in looked oddly familiar. I couldn't think why, until I realised I was opposite the mansion block of flats where Grace and Joshua lived.

I wondered whether they'd mind me turning up on the doorstep and decided they probably wouldn't. After all, Grace had said on my birthday that I could go and cry on her shoulder at any time: and I supposed this qualified as crying on her shoulder. They'll probably be out, anyway, I thought, as I rang the doorbell.

But they weren't. Grace herself answered the door. She was dressed in a sort of kaftan thing and her feet were bare. She had a glass of wine in one hand.

"Lizzie!" she exclaimed when she saw me. "What a lovely surprise! Well, don't just stand there - come on in!"

I took one look at her smiling, welcoming face and I couldn't help myself. I just burst into tears.

They ushered me in and sat me down, and Joshua gave me a box of Kleenex and made me a mug of tea. I told them all about it - Oaklands, and Amber and Camilla, and the liver and the disco - it was so lovely to have sympathetic listeners to all the things I'd been bottling up inside me for the past month or so. They nodded at all the right places.

Joshua laughed about the liver. He said: "I think I've seen that Amber creature around - does she live locally?"

I nodded. "I think so."

"I thought as much - proper little tart, she looks."

Grace frowned. "Joshua! - such language!" I didn't mind the language. His comment reminded me of Mrs Morris - it was just the sort of thing she would say.

Anyway, Grace telephoned Daddy and told him I was there with them, and not to come and collect me. Then Joshua drove me home. I felt better for having unburdened myself, I must say. I asked Grace not to tell Daddy or Miss Bullock what I'd said, and she agreed.

"It'll be *our* secret," she said, "and don't forget - you can come and confide in me any time you like." I didn't want to confide in Daddy: I wanted him to think I could cope, I suppose. Joshua and I concocted some story to tell Daddy about seeing me outside the disco as he drove by, and asking me round to see Grace. I didn't like deceiving Daddy. But it was important that I managed Amber on my own.

I wondered what she had up her sleeve for me next.

5

Jacob and Emma

But things at school seemed to quieten down a bit after that – things with Amber Delaney, I mean. In an odd sort of way, I was quite sorry. It had given me something to think about, something to take my mind off Daddy and Miss Bullock, and being in London instead of Cornwall. But now Amber seemed to have given up her campaign against me (although for how long I didn't know), my thoughts turned necessarily to my changed circumstances.

We'd been in London now for a couple of months and I dearly missed my friends and our lovely little cottage in Cornwall. I missed seeing Meg and Charles and Katey, and singing in the church choir. I missed Maudie, and Ben, even though I hadn't seen much of him since he'd gone away to school. But most of all, I missed Cornwall itself – the little roads half-hidden between the hedges, foaming with May-blossom and hawthorn this time of year; the white-capped breakers beating themselves into oblivion against the proud high cliffs; the whitewashed seagulls turning endlessly in the blue, blue sky. I ached inside with the missing of it all.

I'd taken to going for long walks on Barnes Common, now I knew my way a little better, taking Rufus for company. It was a poor substitute for the Cornish cliffs, but it was outside, and there were trees and grass. I got to recognise other people walking their dogs – it was almost a kind of club. Apart from giving Rufus his exercise, the walks served to get me out of the house. I really couldn't bear being around Daddy and Miss Bullock. They were still mooning around each other, holding hands and stuff, and I felt uncomfortable and unwanted. And with Daddy still working at home, and Miss Bullock not having found another teaching job yet, they were both around an awful lot. So I just stayed out as much as I could.

I had also started taking money from Miss Bullock's purse more regularly – that pound for the disco had

started it all off. I knew she could afford it: she had piles of money, or at least her parents did. Anyway, it wasn't much each time – just 50p or a pound. Funny, but I never took anything from Daddy's wallet, although he left it lying around. It didn't seem right. But I didn't care about taking from *Her* – I didn't think of it as stealing.

Once, when I'd seen a music book I wanted to buy in Richmond, I took five pounds from her purse. That did worry me when I thought about it later. I didn't see how she could fail to miss that much. But I couldn't put it back: that was far too risky.

Sure enough, she discovered the loss and, to make it worse, I was in the room when she did so. It was a Saturday morning and the milkman had called to be paid.

"That's funny," said Miss Bullock, rummaging through her purse. "I put the money here, especially – here, in this zipped compartment." That was where I'd taken it from.

"Are you sure?" asked Daddy.

"Positive. *You'll* have to pay him, Jamie: he's waiting on the doorstep."

When Daddy came back from paying the milkman, Miss Bullock was still turning her purse and her handbag inside out, looking for the missing money.

"This is most odd," she was saying. "It's not the first time it's happened, either – remember the pound you gave me that disappeared? You know, the one for the Scouts' sponsored swim."

Daddy creased his brow in perplexity. "Yes, I remember. But who can have taken it? We've not had any strangers in the house."

Miss Bullock turned to me. "Lizzie?" she said. I expect she was only going to ask me if I'd seen any strangers around, but I went red. I could feel myself growing hot.

"*I* didn't take it," I said loudly. "Don't accuse *me!*"

"Nobody's accusing you of anything," said Daddy gently.

"*She* was going to," I said, pointing a finger at Miss Bullock. "*She* was going to ask me if I'd taken it. Well, I haven't," I lied.

Daddy looked at me with distaste. It was horrid – there was such disgust in that look. It wasn't my fault – I hadn't known the money was for the milkman or the Scouts. I wouldn't have taken it if I'd known – of course I wouldn't.

It didn't stop me, though, over the following weeks: I carried on, taking 50p here, 75p there. I was just more careful, that was all.

Something else that happened during this time was that I started violin lessons at last. My new teacher was a friend of Miss Berkowitz (my music teacher at Oaklands). The violin teacher's name was Mr Owen. He was Welsh, and had a softly musical voice. I could have listened to that voice all lesson: it was beautiful.

Mr Owen lived in Barnes too. He taught during the day at a music school which sounded very interesting: it was called the Central London School of Music. The pupils did proper lessons too – like History and Maths – but they spent a large part of each day studying and playing music. It sounded wonderful – I'd have loved the chance to go to a school like that, instead of rotten horrible Oaklands. Mr Owen said he'd speak to my parents about it, but I said there was no point. I knew Daddy wouldn't let me go to CLSM (as Mr Owen called it): he wanted me to go to the school Miss Bullock had chosen. He was always banging on about what a marvellous place Oaklands was.

All the same, Mr Owen was a very good teacher. I enjoyed my lessons. He had a way of explaining things that made them seem perfect sense, and a way of making me play things that I'd thought impossible. My violin lessons were the only thing about Barnes I really enjoyed.

The spring days lengthened into summer, and July was upon us – hot and dusty and thirst-making. The overgrown garden was a mass of blowsy roses, out of which the bees stumbled, drunk with nectar. I was leaving my bedroom window open at night and I would fall asleep smelling the thick scent of the honeysuckle which grew under it.

It was the time of year for lazing around, not going to school. My thirsty skin craved a dip in the sea at Penwithin Strand. I was going to Cornwall for the holidays as soon as school broke up in the middle of the month. I couldn't wait.

One evening, a couple of weeks before the end of term, the telephone rang while we were having supper.

"I'll get it," I said, standing up. I was half-expecting Pippa to ring, to arrange a few more practice sessions before she left school for good.

It wasn't Pippa. It was Charles. He was ringing from a call-box – I could hear him feeding the coins in. He sounded most odd – flustered and unlike his usual self.

"Is that you, Wendy?" was the first thing he said.

"No," I said, my mouth full of Scotch egg, "it's me – Lizzie. D'you want to speak to her?"

"No – no, that's OK, Lizzie. I'll talk to you – that's fine."

"Whatever's the matter?" I asked him. "You sound most peculiar."

"Do I?" He giggled - *giggled*! Vicars don't giggle: I knew there was something funny going on. Then he hiccupped. "Oh, sorry, Lizzie - I've been drinking a drop of whisky. One of the other fathers in the hospital had a bottle - he insisted on sharing it with me."

"Fathers? Hospital?" I didn't know what he was on about: for a wild moment I thought he meant fathers as in clergymen and had a mental picture of a gang of giggling, hiccupping vicars passing round a bottle of whisky.

"It's Meg, you see," Charles went on, "She's here, in the hospital. It's the baby."

My stomach suddenly lurched into my throat. Meg's baby wasn't due for about another six weeks - something must have gone wrong. "What's *happened*?" I asked. "Why's she in hospital? Is the baby all right?"

Daddy and Miss Bullock, hearing my words, came hurriedly to where I was standing in the hall, phone clasped to my ear.

But Charles was off again. "All right? I should say so - just decided to come into the world a week or so early, that's all. It seems Meg got the dates mixed up - the first thing I knew about it was a telephone call from the hospital when I was at the Deanery. By the time I got here, it was all over - I was a father again!"

"Well, what is it?" I asked eagerly.

"You've got a nephew, Lizzie - Meg's given me a beautiful, bouncing son! His name's Jacob - just you wait till you see him!"

"Heavens!" I breathed. I was awed by the whole thing. "Meg's had her baby," I said to Daddy. "It's a boy - here, you'd better speak to Charles." I passed him the phone.

Mother and baby both doing well, Daddy reported

back. He was dead chuffed at having a grandson, I could see that.

"I've arranged with Charles that Wendy and I will drive you down to Penlorren when you break up," said Daddy. "That way, we can see our new grandson. We'll stay over for a couple of days, then drive back."

I was pleased – I had originally been going down by train, which meant leaving Rufus and Fishpaste behind. Cornwall wouldn't have been the same without them.

"Oh goody," I said, "we can take the animals with us."

"No, we can't," said Daddy firmly. "We can't keep dragging them up and down to Cornwall and back: the poor things won't know where home is."

"But, Daddy," I said anxiously, "We've *got* to. Otherwise who'll feed them, and look after them, and take Rufus for his walks?" There was a silence. Daddy looked at Miss Bullock.

"She's got a point, you know, Jamie," she said to Daddy. "We can't just leave them here on their own."

"All right," said Daddy. "We'll take them with us – *if* Meg and Charles don't mind. They may, you know, with a new baby in the house."

"Don't be stupid," I said scornfully. "They didn't mind them when *Katey* was little."

"If you carry on speaking to me like that," said Daddy, "the animals will stay here. Full stop."

"Oh, do let's take them," I wailed. "I can easily manage them on the train coming home – I know I can. I won't have much else to carry – oh, please, Daddy. I'll miss them so much otherwise. They'll miss me too – refuse to eat, probably."

"Don't kid yourself," said Daddy. "They're far too greedy for that. You can't possibly manage them both, on your own, with all your other luggage. They'll come back with Wendy and me in the car, and that's an end to it."

I didn't want an end to it. "Oh Daddy," I said petulantly. "Why are you so mean? You know you don't care about the animals." I meant he didn't care about them in the same way as I did, but it didn't come out like that.

Daddy was cross. "You seem to forget Rufus is actually *my* dog," he said.

"He loves me more than you," I muttered sulkily.

"While we're on the subject," Daddy went on, "can't you do something about that cat of yours? He rampages around as though he owns the place. He seems to have a predilection for putting muddy pawprints all over my papers."

"*And* over your sheets," put in Miss Bullock. I stared at her. "Does he really have to sleep on your bed? I'm sure it's not hygienic. I'll buy him a basket."

I was furious. "Of course he's got to sleep with me!" I shouted. Fishpaste sleep in a basket? – it was unthinkable. "He's always slept on my bed – he'll be confused if you make him stop!"

"That's enough!" shouted Daddy. "The cat's a wretched nuisance, Lizzie – and you encourage him. And Rufus – he's become totally out of control! I don't know what things are coming to. They'll stay here, and that's final."

"Jamie," said Miss Bullock softly. "Don't let's quarrel – not after getting such happy news about Meg and Charles and the baby. Let's decide about the pets nearer the time."

But I think Daddy felt like quarrelling. He left off about Rufus and Fishpaste, but started on about church. Charles' telephone call had reminded him that I hadn't been going lately.

"After having sung in the church choir, too," he said. "You never missed a service. You ought to start going again." I pointed out that he and Miss Bullock didn't go either.

"That's beside the point," he said. He was getting cross again.

"Why?" I wanted to know. "Anyway, I don't believe in God any more. I don't believe God would have let all this happen to me – moving away from Cornwall and everything. And if He did, I don't want to believe in Him."

Daddy told me I was ungrateful then – ungrateful and a heathen. I told him he was being unChristian to Rufus and Fishpaste, and rushed off to the Common with Rufus.

The Saturday before we broke up, Harriet's eldest sister Emma was eighteen and had a birthday party. Harriet invited me, which surprised and pleased me, and Amber wasn't invited, which pleased me even more.

The party was to be a posh affair, with a hired band (a 'five-piece', Harriet said), a hundred guests and a buffet supper, and it was to be at a dead swish hotel. Miss Bullock suggested I wore my bridesmaid's dress – the invitation said 'Black tie' at the bottom, which she explained meant ladies had to wear dressy clothes. Why it couldn't just say 'Dressy Clothes' I don't know. Grown-ups always seem to speak in some sort of code.

Anyway, Daddy was in a jolly mood for once when he drove me to the hotel. "Have a good time, sweetie," he said as he did his chauffeur bit, opening my door. To my relief, I saw Pippa just about to go in.

"Hello, Lizzie," she said. "Let's go in together, shall we? It's awful on your own."

Once inside we found Harriet, who introduced me to

her parents and her sisters - Sophie, who'd invited Pippa, and Emma, the birthday girl. She looked very happy. She was holding hands with a handsome man with thick brown hair and hazel eyes.

"That's Jonathan," whispered Harriet to me. "They're unofficially engaged."

We danced around for a bit and then the supper was served. It was delicious - it reminded me of Daddy's wedding, even more so when a large pink birthday cake was produced. Emma cut it and thanked all the guests for coming and for all the presents she'd had. All the older ones had glasses of champagne, but we had to make do with fizzy orange - it tasted like Lucozade.

It was shortly after that when things started going wrong - wrong for me, that is. Harriet and Pippa and me and some others were dancing madly, and when we finished I was terribly thirsty. I looked around for my glass, but it had gone. Somebody must have taken it, I thought.

"What's wrong?" asked a male voice. It was one of Emma's friends, I think. "Lost your drink? Here, have this one." He passed me a full glass.

I must have looked dubious.

"It's OK," he said, "it's only fruit juice."

I was parched and drank it down in one long gulp. It was delicious: nectar, ambrosia - like nothing I'd ever tasted before. When I'd finished it, I didn't want to dance any more; I just wanted to sit there.

Then Harriet came over. "Come on, Lizzie," she said, "don't be lazy - come and dance!" I stood up - and nearly fell over. I felt dizzy and all the dancing couples were multiplied in a crazy kaleidoscope of colour and swirling sound. I giggled helplessly: I suddenly felt very happy and carefree.

"What are you waiting for? Let's go and dance!" I said. At least, that's what I wanted to say, but I couldn't seem to get my tongue round the words. I don't know when Harriet realised there was something wrong with me: I danced like a whirling dervish, laughing and shrieking. People had to make room for me as I bumped into them like an out-of-control dodgem car.

All of a sudden, I felt horribly sick and dizzy. I stopped dancing and stumbled off the dance floor.

Harriet came with me. "What's wrong, Lizzie?" she asked anxiously.

"I feel ill," I muttered.

She looked at me with interest. "I say, you're not drunk, are you?"

I didn't see how I could be – I'd only had the Lucozade. Then I remembered: that drink the boy had given me! It must have been alcoholic, and I'd drunk it down like lemonade. Waves of nausea flowed over me. "I'm going to be sick," I gasped.

"Come outside, into the fresh air," urged Harriet, "it might help."

But it didn't. As the fresh air hit me, my tummy turned over in protest and I was sick all down the front of my bridesmaid's dress. I felt ghastly, and started to cry weakly.

"I want to go home," I sobbed, "I want Daddy. I want to go home."

"What on earth's going on?" thundered a familiar voice behind me.

I turned round. It was Daddy, come to take me home.

6

Back to Penwithin

Daddy and Miss Bullock were furious with me – they thought it was my fault, that I'd purposely been drinking at the party. As if I would!

I don't remember much about getting home, only their furious frozen faces and me feeling too ill to tell them what had really happened. I suppose somebody must have undressed me and put me to bed, because when I woke up the next morning I had my nightie on – inside out. That was the least of my problems: my head felt like *it* was on inside out, too. Somebody had set up a steam-hammer inside my brain and my mouth tasted as though Fishpaste had been sleeping in it all night.

In short, I had a hangover – I'd have been interested in it if I hadn't felt so dismal. Miss Bullock came stomping in with a face like a bulldog to give me some Alka Seltzer, and lectured me at ninety million decibels on the evils of drink. She didn't have to tell me: *I* was suffering them, not her. I groaned and rolled over.

"Honestly, Lizzie," she said, exasperated. "Whatever has got into you? Oh, well, I suppose you'd better stay in bed this morning."

"Go away and let me die in peace," I moaned. She slammed the door spitefully on her way out.

I slept on and off for the rest of the morning, dreaming odd dreams about seagulls and Amber and Meg's new baby. Then Daddy came into the bedroom, looking concerned and caring, and not at all cross. He told me that Harriet's mother had just rung to see how I was feeling.

"How did she know about it?" I asked. I felt a bit better.

"Well," he said, "a young chap rang her this morning – one of Emma's friends, apparently. He was feeling guilty about having tricked one of Harriet's friends into drinking a cocktail – said she knocked it back in one go. Mrs Smith checked with Harriet, and Harriet said it must be you. So she rang to make sure you were all right."

So now Daddy and Miss Bullock knew the truth.

"Why didn't you tell us?" Miss Bullock gently asked me later.

"I felt too ill last night – and by this morning you were convinced it was my fault. I didn't think you'd believe me." I felt maligned and virtuous, all at once.

"The thing is," said Daddy, "the way things have been just lately, we thought you were – well, attention-seeking. Sorry we misjudged you, Lizzie."

They were really nice to me after that, for at least a week. They felt guilty, I suppose. But I really don't know how grown-ups cope with drinking if it makes you feel like that afterwards.

21st July

Dear Diary,
At last! – I'm in Cornwall. I'm in my usual room at the vicarage and I can hear the sea very faintly. I'd forgotten

you can hear it from here: I miss the sound of the sea, in Barnes.

Daddy and Miss Bullock have stopped treating me like breakable china. Daddy well and truly stopped today when he was loading up the car with all the luggage. He loathes doing it and was in a bad mood. He got in an even worse one when I remembered, half way to the M3, that we'd left Fishpaste behind. Daddy wanted to leave him, but Miss Bullock made him turn round and go back. Poor Fishpaste: he was in his travelling basket, in the middle of the hall, making a dreadful din. He thought we'd deserted him. But Daddy ended up pleased we'd gone back, because he discovered he'd left the back door unlocked. We'd probably have been burgled if he'd left it like that. We got here a bit late. Charles was pleased to see us. Meg comes home with Jacob tomorrow. I can't wait to see them both.

Mrs Morris had been staying at the vicarage while Meg was in hospital, to look after Charles and Katey. Meg had had to stay in for a bit longer than usual, Charles said: the doctor wanted to keep an eye on them both on account of Jacob arriving a bit early.

It was great to see Mrs Morris again. She looked more lugubrious than ever. "You've put on weight, me lad," she said to Daddy. She did insist on seeing him as a lad. "That's what married life does for you. You been feeding him up, duck?" she asked Miss Bullock who preened and simpered.

The next day, Charles went to the hospital to fetch Meg and the baby. Meg came through the front door holding Jacob, who was wrapped up in a snowy shawl and sound asleep. She beamed proudly. The effect was magical.

Katey stopped banging her spoon on her high-chair. Miss Bullock and Mrs Morris said "aahh" in fond tones. Daddy swallowed hard and I could see his eyes misting over. I just stood and looked – Jacob looked so tiny and sweet, asleep in his mother's arms.

Meg looked round at us all, still beaming. She stepped towards me. "Here, Lizzie," she said. "Hold him for me." She placed him in my arms.

I looked down at my tiny nephew and my heart swelled with love and pride. Suddenly, his cornflower blue eyes opened and his rosy lips parted. "Look," I breathed. "Look – he's smiling at me!"

"It's wind," said Mrs Morris and everybody laughed.

But I'm sure he was smiling and I'll never forget that moment as long as I live.

That afternoon I went to see Maudie. It was good to see her. Ben wasn't due home until next week.

Maudie's voice seemed more Scottish than ever. We danced around each other with glee. "Will you come and sing in the choir tomorrow?" she asked me. "Do say you will! I've told Mr Trotter you're back for the holidays."

"You actually spoke to him, then?" I teased.

She went red. "Och, well, not exactly. I got Beth to tell him." Beth was a bit older than us, and brazen. She'd say anything to anyone for a dare.

Then Maudie told me her mother was back in hospital. "She doesn't seem ill exactly – just tired and restless. I go to see her most days."

"I expect she'll be out soon," I told her. "I'll come with you some times, if you like."

"Would you?" Maudie's eyes shone. "She'd like that – aye, she'd like that. She doesn't get many visitors apart from me and my father."

"Oh, I'm so glad to be back!" I sang happily. "We'll have such lovely holidays – once Ben's back, it'll be just like old times!" I began to tell her all about Barnes and Amber, and how awful it all was.

Daddy and Miss Bullock went back to London the day Ben was due home. That morning Daddy brought me a cup of tea. He was in his dressing gown. It was very early: they wanted to make a good start, he said. He sat at the foot of my bed and stroked Fishpaste. He seemed oddly ill at ease – I guess he wanted to tell me something.

"How do you like your new nephew, then?" he asked me.

"He's great," I said, dipping a digestive biscuit into the tea.

"How would you feel about a new brother or sister?" The end of the biscuit fell off into the tea. I hardly noticed it.

"How do you mean?" I asked suspiciously. But I knew what Daddy was going to say before he said it.

"Wendy's going to have a baby – isn't that marvellous?" I didn't think it at all marvellous. I put the tea down.

"But you've only been married three months!" I burst out. "You didn't waste any time, did you?"

"Lizzie!" Daddy said, looking shocked. "Don't be like that! We're thrilled about it. Wendy had been told she could never have any children, you see, so this is a double surprise."

I felt vaguely disgusted. To my mind, there was something odd about Daddy going to be a father again, after just meeting his baby grandson.

I shuddered. "I think it's disgusting," I said, "at your

age. I thought you'd given up that sort of thing when Mummy died."

There was a silence; then Daddy covered my hand with his own large, rough one. "Lizzie," he sighed, "oh, Lizzie. What must we do to make you like and accept her? Can't you see she makes me happy – doesn't that make *you* happy, even a tiny bit? To see your old Dad young and laughing again?"

I looked into his eyes. They seemed full of a deep sadness. The moment seemed to go on forever and I was nearly swayed. I nearly threw my arms round his dear old neck and told him I was glad for him. But I didn't. I steeled myself and looked away.

"No," I said cruelly. "I think it's disgusting."

The moment was broken. Daddy left the room and I stayed in bed until 11 o'clock, not even getting up to say goodbye to them when they left.

I thought of this new baby. They would be all over it when it arrived – they'd forget about me. It would be as though I didn't exist. Well, I do exist, I told myself firmly, and right now I'm here where I want to be – in Cornwall. I *will* enjoy these holidays; I will, I will.

When I saw Ben, I stared. I couldn't help it – he'd grown about six inches in the three months since I'd last seen him. Something had happened to his face, too – I can't explain it. It looked harder, more angular, somehow. He looked less like a boy than a man. Of course, he'd be fifteen soon. His voice had changed as well. It was no longer squeaky. It was deep and smooth, like brown velvet. Just occasionally, it would go up at the end of a sentence.

I felt quite shy of this new, grown-up Ben. He thought I'd changed, too.

"You look more – sort of ..." he made curving gestures with his hands. He walked round me. "Your hair's longer. You've got a spot on your chin."

"OK, OK, I know," I snapped. "You'll get spots too, soon – I bet you will!"

"Your voice is different," he said accusingly.

"So's yours," I rejoined.

"Mine's just broken – at last," he said offhandedly. "Yours is *different*. Posher – like a grockle's."

"It's not!" I said hotly. But I think it was. Early on at Oaklands, stung by the "Ooh-aar Oliver" taunts, I'd made an effort to iron out some of the Cornish vowels. I hadn't thought I'd succeeded, but Ben obviously did.

When we met Maudie, she and Ben stared at each other wordlessly. A red flush deepened on Maudie's cheeks. I'd had my suspicions before about Maudie, that she fancied Ben, and this seemed to confirm them. I couldn't understand what she saw in him to fancy – he was only Ben, after all.

But this seemed to set the tone for the whole of the holidays: Ben and Maudie were together and I was trailing around after them. It made me cross: they were *my* friends first, after all. But they didn't seem to care if I was with them or not. They weren't unkind to me – I was always included in their plans, to go swimming, on a picnic, shrimping. Once we all went to visit Maudie's mother in hospital. I was shocked when I saw her – she seemed to have shrunk, her face was white and sunken on the pillow. I didn't know how Maudie could say she didn't look ill.

After a while, I took to going for walks on the cliffs with just Rufus for company. I'd been so looking forward to coming back to Cornwall: I'd been ticking off the days in my diary. But now I was here, things just weren't turning out the way I'd planned. I tried hard to enjoy myself, really I did, but it was hard when I had to listen to Ben and Maudie going on interminably about school and TV and life, and whether the moon was made of green cheese, like as not.

I told them about London and Oaklands and how gruesome it was. I told them about Miss Bullock and the new baby. I told them about being ignored at school, and Amber and the liver, and the party when I'd got accidentally drunk. They listened politely enough, and said "yes" and "no" and "how horrid" in all the right places, but they weren't really interested, I could tell. I felt let down and unwanted. I felt cheated. But most of all, I felt jealous, jealous of them both. They were *my* friends first. How dare they usurp each other?

All in all, I wasn't much enjoying the holidays. But one day, when the three of us were supposed to be taking a picnic up onto the cliffs at Penlyn Point, Maudie didn't turn up at Ben's house where we'd planned to meet.

"She phoned just before you got here," said Ben from the kitchen, rolling his swimming trunks in his towel. His Mum was cutting egg-and-tomato sandwiches on the scarred wooden table. "She's got to go and see her Mum – she had a bad night, Maudie said."

"Poor Mrs Campbell," I said. Inwardly, my heart soared, and I felt a bit ashamed of myself. I could have Ben all to myself today – yippee! "Never mind – we'll have a nice time on our own."

"Mind you enjoy yourselves, my dears," called Mrs Polkerris from the back door, waving a tea towel. She *was* nice. She'd given us chocolate and saffron cake from the shop before we left. My spirits rose: it was a glorious August day. The sun was shining, the temperature rising, and I could stay in Cornwall for the rest of the holidays.

Daddy had rung the vicarage the night before, saying Miss Bullock's parents had invited them both to stay with them at their villa in Greece, and would I mind staying on in Cornwall another three weeks?

Would I *mind*! - you try and stop me, I thought, as Ben and I climbed up the cliff path. When we reached our destination, we changed into our swimming things - Ben modestly, behind a towel, now he considered himself grown up - and skittered on our behinds down the broad rock fissure to the small, secret cove below.

We swam around for ages in the clear green water, smooth as bath oil, until we started getting cold. Then we climbed back the way we'd come, up the rocks and the granite slabs of broken cliff, to the top. We spread our towels on the grass and lay down to dry in the sun. I found myself telling him all about my problems again - but it all seemed to come out wrong. Instead of just telling him, I went on and on, like a scratched record.

"Honestly, Ben," I heard myself whine, "you've no idea how awful it is to be ignored." I'd temporarily forgotten that *he'd* been ignored, too, when he'd started at his school. "That Amber Delaney - but I'll get her. I'll stop her tricks." I waited for Ben's comment, but he didn't make one. I went on.

"And fancy *Her* going to have a baby - I think that's disgusting, don't you? Her and my father - yuck!" Still no answer. I wondered if he was asleep. "I hate Barnes - it's horrible. And that dreadful Oaklands place. Nobody asked *me* about it - nobody bothered to find out *my* feelings. They just went ahead. They don't care about me."

"They probably knew what you'd say," came Ben's voice suddenly.

I was startled. "Wh - what?" I asked. "What did you say?"

I looked at Ben. He sat up. "They probably didn't ask you how you felt because they knew what you'd say," he repeated.

I had a horrid feeling I'd gone on too much. But I couldn't stop now. "Oh yes," I challenged, "and what's that?"

"That you didn't like it - the same way you haven't liked anything your Dad's done since he told you they were getting married." Ben's voice was sarcastic.

I was stunned. He was supposed to be my *friend* - supposed to be on my side.

He went on. "*Nobody understands me!*" He mocked my voice. "*Everybody's against me! They're all trying to upset me!*"

I was suddenly furious with him. "It's all right for you," I burst out. "*Your* life's still nice and cosy. *Your* mother's still alive - *your* Dad's not marrying another woman and moving you away!"

"Why don't you grow up?" Ben shouted at me. "You're so selfish - all you ever think about is you. Why can't you think about how your Dad feels about it - have you ever thought about how *he* feels, with you acting like a spoilt two-year-old?"

I could barely speak with rage. How had he the nerve to criticize me, after he and Maudie had ignored me all summer? "It's better than acting like Rufus when he goes after a dog in heat!"

Ben went very quiet. "What's that supposed to mean?" he demanded. I'd never seen him like this before - cold and angry. He almost frightened me.

"You know what I mean," I muttered. "You and Maudie ..."

"You leave Maudie out of this," he said, very quietly.

"I don't want to leave her out of it - and anyway, it's

me who's been left out," I said childishly.

"You really are self-obsessed, aren't you?" shouted Ben, suddenly loud again. "How do you think Maudie feels, with you and your continual moaning about poor you and your wicked stepmother? Maudie envies you your family – she won't have a mother soon."

I didn't understand. "What do you mean?" I said, puzzled. "Maudie's *got* a mother – you know she has."

"But she's dying – *dying*!" Ben yelled. "She's got cancer, and she's dying, and what's more Maudie knows it." His voice carried around the still air.

I don't know what made me continue – I suppose I wanted the last word.

"My mother died too," I said smugly. "She'll get over it."

Ben shot me a look of pure hatred and disgust. He pulled his shorts on over his trunks and shoved his towel in his bag.

"Where are you going?" I asked him, suddenly worried.

"Home," he said through his teeth. "I don't want to be with you any more. You make me feel ill." And he picked up his bag and was gone.

I sat on the cliffs, in the beautiful summer sunshine, and wept with shame and guilt and horror.

7

Disaster for Rufus

The rest of the holidays were awful. I stayed away from Ben and Maudie for the remaining week or so and they stayed away from me. I spent the time alone in my room or going for long solitary walks, and if Meg and Charles thought it odd they didn't say anything. They were busy, anyway: Charles with his usual vicar-like work, Meg with fitting Jacob into her routine. It's amazing how much time a new baby takes up and that filled me with gloom too, much as I loved Jacob. I could just see all Daddy's and Miss Bullock's time being taken up with their new baby, when it arrived. Not that I wanted *Her* time, of course.

Going back to Barnes on the train after the holidays was one of the low points of my life. I felt utterly dejected – homeless, rootless. I fitted in nowhere. The only thing that had kept me going in Barnes was the memory of Cornwall, looking forward to going back. Now even that was spoilt. Nothing would ever be the same again.

It was a chilly, wet September, which suited the way I

felt. Three weeks into term, I received a cold little note from Ben.

Dear Lizzie (it said),
Maudie's mother died yesterday. I thought you'd like to know. You might write to Maudie, or something. I reckon she's feeling pretty awful.
From Ben.

That was it – no "with love", no "I hope you're well", nothing. Just the bare facts. I ached inside for our lost friendship, and for Maudie. I couldn't bear to keep that stiff letter, so I crumpled it up and threw it away. I will write to her though, I told myself. I promise I will.

Two days later, Charles rang to tell me when Mrs Campbell's funeral was – he was conducting it.

"I thought you might like to send some flowers," he said. "How's Maudie taking it?"

He obviously thought that, being Maudie's friend, I knew all about it: he didn't know I hadn't spoken to her for over a month. I thought I'd better come clean.

"I don't know," I managed to get out. "I haven't spoken to her for ages."

Charles, being kind, and sensitive to these things, didn't ask me why not. He just said, very gently, "You did know she'd died, didn't you, Lizzie?"

I had a big lump in my throat. I nodded, then realised Charles couldn't see me.

"Yes," I croaked.

"Who told you?" he asked, gently.

I felt unbearably sad.

"Ben," I said, my voice barely there. "He wrote."

There was a pause while Charles digested all this. Then: "Would you like me to give Maudie a message from you – when I see her?" he asked me.

"Yes," I said, "yes, please. Tell her ..." but I couldn't think of anything to say.

Another pause.

"I'll tell her your thoughts are with her, shall I? And that you'll be in touch?"

"Yes, please. I've got to go now – give my love to Meg and everyone," and I put the phone down in a rush.

I was flooded with memories of when my own mother died. After the first day or so of phone calls and people paying their respects, everybody stayed away. I knew they were only trying to be kind – giving us time to be on our own, to "get over it" – but it was the worst thing about it. It was as though we ceased to exist for a few weeks.

I sat on the stairs and put my face in my hands. I'll write to Maudie tonight, I thought. And while I'm about it, I'll write to Ben, too. I don't want to drift out of his life. I'll write and tell him I'm sorry.

Somehow, I felt much better when I'd decided to do that. I told Daddy about Mrs Campbell, and Miss Bullock met me from school the next day and took me to the florist to order some flowers. She arranged for some more flowers to be sent from her and Daddy. When we got back, she made some tea and we sat in the kitchen together to drink it. Daddy had gone out somewhere. It was cosy in the kitchen.

"Horrid things, funerals," she said musingly, gazing into her teacup.

I nodded. I remembered Mummy's – a freezing cold December wind, and the ground so hard it could barely be dug; and all the flowers, bright and cheerful and mocking on the white snow, brazenly alive while my mother was dead in that cold cold ground.

I clasped my hands round the hot tea in the mug.

"Poor Maudie," I said.

"Poor Maudie," agreed Miss Bullock, "and poor Mr Campbell. Don't be sad for Maudie's mother, Lizzie – she was very ill, and in a lot of pain. It was a merciful release for her." That's what Charles had said. I wondered if Maudie thought so.

As if she read my thoughts, Miss Bullock said, "It's Maudie and her Dad who need the support now – write to her, Lizzie, and tell her you understand how she's feeling," she urged.

"I will," I promised, "I'll do it this evening." We sat in silence. I felt almost close to her then: it's funny how death seemed to have closed the gap between us a little.

After that, things seemed oddly brighter. I must be funny, I thought, being cheered up by people dying and things. But I knew it wasn't that exactly. It was rather that Mrs Campbell's death had set things off – a catalyst, I think it's called. A little light had started to burn inside me, a little light which made me want to set out and improve things for myself, instead of waiting around for them to get better by themselves. It sounds peculiar, I know, but that's the only way I can describe it.

So I wrote to Maudie and to Ben. It was hard to know what to say to Maudie. I asked Miss Bullock what she thought I should write, and she seemed pleased I'd asked her. She also suggested I might invite Maudie to stay for half-term, so I did.

Ben's letter was even harder to write. I apologised for being such a pig in the holidays and told him I'd written to Maudie – it was a very short letter.

They both replied almost by return, Maudie saying

how much she appreciated my letter and she'd love to come for half-term; Ben's full of rugger scores and reports on the school food. I knew I was back in his good books then.

I felt much happier after that. Things were looking up. Then, out of the blue, something happened to turn my new-found peace of mind on its head.

It was a Friday evening, the week before half-term, and I was taking Rufus for his usual run on the Common before going home for tea. It was a beautiful sunny October evening and it was quite warm. I was singing as I walked along. I hadn't done *that* for ages – I usually seemed to be sunk in gloom, head down, trudging along.

Rufus was snuffling around, in and out of the bushes, looking for rabbits. He never caught any – but he never gave up, either. Daddy says he's dogged. I say that's an awful pun.

We'd gone a long way – almost as far as the road which bisects the Common. It was teatime. I whistled for Rufus, and turned to go back. It was such a nice evening I stopped to say hello to a woman I regularly saw walking her dog and we talked for a bit, about the weather and the dogs. After a few minutes, I called Rufus again: we'd be late for our tea if we didn't hurry.

But he didn't appear. I called and whistled, and whistled and called: no Rufus. I was getting a bit worried. Although he wasn't exactly trained to Barbara Woodhouse standards, he usually came when called, especially when it's time for tea.

Suddenly, I heard a squeal of brakes from the road, followed by a yelp. I just knew it was Rufus. I rushed over to the road, dreading what I knew I'd see.

Rufus was lying there in the road, motionless, his

beautiful blond head in a pool of his own blood. His right front leg was at a curious angle. I knew he was dead.

A youngish man was getting out of a car which had pulled up on to the verge. He ran over to where I was crouching over Rufus, silent tears pouring down my face.

"He just came rushing out into the road," panted the man. He looked upset. "I couldn't avoid him – honestly, love, he just rushed out."

"Rufus," I sobbed, "oh Rufus."

"I'm sorry, love," said the man. He looked near to tears himself. "Oh God – I feel awful about this." I bent further over Rufus' inert body. I couldn't speak.

"Look, love, we'd better move him – we can't leave him here on the road."

"Leave him alone!" I scrambled to my feet. "Don't you dare touch him!"

The man bent down over Rufus, then knelt on the road, his head against the dog's side.

"Hang on a tick – he's breathing. Yes, he's definitely breathing."

I hopped from foot to foot in anguish. A little crowd was beginning to gather. My only thought was to fetch Daddy. Daddy would take care of everything; he'd make sure Rufus was all right.

"Stay here," I gasped, "I'm going to get Daddy." I rushed off, leaving the man still listening to Rufus' side and saying "definitely breathing".

I don't know how I got back to the house. It was like one of those awful dreams when, however hard you run, you stay on the same spot. Eventually I threw open the back door. My lungs felt rough and raw with the effort, my breath coming in great ragged gasps. Miss Bullock was washing a lettuce at the sink and turned round in alarm when she heard me.

"Lizzie!" she said. "What's happened – what's wrong?" I shook my head and tried to get my breath back. She came over to me and put her wet hands on my shoulders.

"Here," she said calmly. "Sit down. Catch your breath." I shook my head again: I couldn't sit down, it would waste time. I had to get back to Rufus.

"Daddy," I managed to gasp. "Where's Daddy?"

She looked momentarily surprised. "Why – he's gone up to Town today, to see his publisher. Don't you remember?"

I'd forgotten. Miss Bullock would have to do.

I grasped her hand and pulled her towards the back door.

"Come on," I panted, "you've got to come – Rufus – he's been run over – on the Common road."

She came immediately, pulling off her apron with one hand and throwing it on the floor. We ran hand in hand over the rough tussocks of the Common until at last we reached the road where Rufus lay. The man with the car was still watching over him.

Rufus had his eyes open. They were full of pain and patience and infinite trust. I put my hand down to touch his velvet nose and his tongue came out and weakly licked my wrist, once. It broke my heart.

Miss Bullock took charge.

"I just didn't see him," the man was still saying.

"Never mind that," she said, "we've got to get him to a vet. Would you take us in your car?"

"Of course," said the man, getting up. You could see he was glad to do something to help. "Of course I will. You'll have to direct me though."

Between them, Miss Bullock and the man gently moved Rufus on to a tartan rug from the man's car. Then they lifted the whole thing and put Rufus on to the back seat. I sat next to him, my hand gently stroking his nose. Miss Bullock sat in front and gave the man directions to the vet's.

"Are you sisters?" asked the man, concentrating on the road. I could tell he was a careful driver. I didn't blame him, not really.

"She's my stepdaughter," answered Miss Bullock shortly. "Left here, then right."

When we got to the vet's, the man insisted on waiting outside.

"I want to make sure he's okay," he said. "I feel really terrible about this – I've got a dog myself, a labrador. I know how I'd be if ... you know ..." he trailed off lamely.

If someone had run over *him*, I finished silently.

The vet cleaned up Rufus' cut eyebrow – it was quite a small cut, really, for such a lot of blood. He stitched it up expertly. He gently examined Rufus all over – Rufus just lay there, quietly brave. Then the vet gave him an injection, and set the front leg in plaster.

He patted the dog's shoulder.

"All done, old fellow," he said cheerfully. "No internal injuries," he said to Miss Bullock. "Just the broken leg, and the cut head, and some concussion. Come back in ten days for me to remove the stitches – the plaster'll be on for a month."

"Will he be all right?" I asked anxiously.

"He should be," replied the vet. "He's young and healthy. There's always some risk, of course – he's had a dreadful shock, and it's usually the shock that's the most dangerous thing. I'll give you some pills for him," he went on. "You'll have to keep your eye on him for a day or two - feed him by hand. He won't feel like much, but make him take something. Baby food, that sort of thing. If he doesn't eat, he'll get very weak and he won't have the strength to get better. If he gets worse, give me a ring and I'll come out to you."

"Thank you very much," I said earnestly.

"Don't worry," the vet said to me kindly. "I've seen animals in much worse states after car accidents than your Rufus here - you wouldn't know anything untoward had happened after a week or so."

I sat up with Rufus all that night, trying to feed him baby food from a spoon. He wouldn't swallow a drop - he just licked some water from my fingers.

All day Saturday I sat with him, trying to make him eat something. It was no good. He just wasn't interested. What was worse, we couldn't get him to take his pills, either: we just couldn't get them down him. He'd never get better if he didn't take his pills or eat - the vet had said so.

We all tried. We all put baby food on our fingers and smeared it round his muzzle, trying to get him to lick it off, but he just let it dry there. He lay stretched out in front of the fire, sleeping, only the rise and fall of his side showing he was still alive. I wondered if he was going to die after all.

At midnight, Daddy and Miss Bullock came downstairs dressed in their night things. I was trying to keep my eyes open.

"You're dead on your feet, Lizzie," said Daddy. "Why don't you go and get some sleep?"

"I've got to look after Rufus," I said, yawning.

"Wendy and I'll do that tonight - we'll do it in shifts.
Go on, sweetie - you'll feel better in the morning and
you'll be able to carry on looking after him then."

I was too tired to argue. Bed suddenly seemed a
wonderful prospect.

"All right," I said. "But you will wake me up if
anything awful happens?"

"Of course we will," they assured me.

I stumbled upstairs, and got under the bedclothes

without even getting undressed. I was asleep almost before I closed my eyes.

I woke up at six o'clock. It was still dark and very quiet. I got out of bed and went downstairs into the sitting room.

Miss Bullock was sitting on the floor in her dressing gown, Rufus' head cradled in her lap. He was licking her fingers. She heard me come in and looked up. The firelight flickered on her face.

"Sshh," she whispered. "I think we've cracked it. I think he's eating."

He was. I dipped my fingers in the saucer of baby food. He licked it off, slowly at first, then greedily. He finished the saucerful.

By eight o'clock, when Daddy came downstairs, Rufus had eaten another saucer of baby food and some cold roast beef Miss Bullock had cut off the joint in the fridge.

"He's going to be all right, isn't he?" I asked Miss Bullock.

She nodded. "I do believe he is."

I flung my arms around her neck: "Oh, thank goodness!"

And that's how Daddy found us when he came into the room.

8

Taken ill

Rufus got gradually better once he started eating again. He kept trying to bite at the plaster cast on his leg. I think he wondered what it was, this hard stiff white thing which stopped him running around. He developed a peculiar dot-and-carry sort of walk – he did look funny. I couldn't help laughing at him and he does so hate being laughed at. He would stop hobbling around and look at me from under his eyebrows in an accusing fashion.

Fishpaste thought it was hilarious, this new white leg Rufus had grown. He soon realised it prevented Rufus from moving quickly and he started to tease him – biting his tail, or sitting on the dresser just out of reach, dangling a paw down and bopping poor Rufus on the nose.

Then it was half-term, and Maudie arrived on the Sunday afternoon. We went to Paddington to collect her. It was the first time she'd been on a train by herself, she said, and she looked rather white.

It was great to see her, though. We drove back to Barnes through the golden autumn light and Maudie told me everything that had been going on at school and church.

"How's Mr Trotter?" I asked. She made a face at the back of Daddy's neck and went red. "What's the matter?" I said.

"Perhaps Maudie doesn't want to tell you all about her love-life with me listening," said Daddy cheerily, meeting her eyes in the driving mirror.

Maudie went even redder. "Och, no, Mr Oliver, that's all right," she stammered. "I don't mind you hearing."

But Daddy didn't get the chance to hear, because at that moment we drew up outside the house. He carried Maudie's suitcases in – it looked as though she'd brought enough for a couple of months.

"Och, haven't you done it all fabulously," she breathed, looking round the hall and peeping into the sitting room.

Miss Bullock came down the stairs in queenly fashion. "Hello, Maudie," she said, holding out her hands. I was a bit surprised at what happened next. Maudie flung her arms round Miss Bullock, greeting her like a long-lost friend.

"Hello," she said. "Och, it's so lovely to be here! It's real nice of you to have invited me!" They beamed at each other with real warmth. I felt a pang of the old jealousy, the jealousy I'd felt in the summer holidays. I struggled with it for several moments.

Then Daddy spoke. "Let's show Maudie her room then, Lizzie," he said. "You've got half an hour to find out all about Mr Trotter before tea."

Of course, that made Maudie blush again, and Miss Bullock said, "Don't tease, Jamie," in mock-severe tones, and the jealousy went away.

I helped Maudie to unpack. "How's your Dad?" I asked

her. It was the nearest I could get to asking how *she* was.

"I think he's OK," she replied, hanging a blouse up. "It was awful at first – well, you know what it's like – but we've talked about it a lot and I think it's helped. It helped to know *you* understood, too." I felt a twinge of guilt at that – I hadn't been very understanding at first, that was for sure. "I hope you didn't mind me with" – she paused – "Miss Bullock just now – you know, hugging her and all that. But she was so kind when my mother was dying, and just after she died – ringing up like that, and the letter she wrote."

I stared at Maudie. "Ringing up? Letter?" I didn't know what she meant. I sat on the bed.

"Yes, you know – when she phoned my father those times – and the letter she wrote, just before you sent yours." Maudie had her back to me and I was glad. I didn't want her to know I'd been unaware of Miss Bullock's thoughtfulness, especially as what *I'd* been feeling at the time was not sympathy but rather murderous jealousy.

"She's very kind, you know." Maudie came and sat beside me. She sighed. "I do miss my mother, though. I know she was suffering and everything, and that's over now, but I miss her so much." I put an awkward arm round Maudie's shoulders. I wasn't used to touching my friends, but I knew Maudie liked it.

"I know," I said quietly. "I still miss mine. But it stops hurting so much after a while. Honestly it does, Maudie."

We sat there like that for a good few minutes, each of us with our own private memories of our mothers, until Miss Bullock called us for tea.

After tea we took Rufus for a walk – or rather, a

hobble - and played cards and Scrabble. Then Maudie and I went upstairs, supposedly to get ready for bed, and ended up in my bedroom talking for ages and ages. She told me that Mr Trotter had fallen by the wayside.

"He's too old for me, anyway," she said. I could hardly believe what I was hearing - I thought she'd sworn undying love for the long-fingered choirmaster.

Then I had a suspicion. "Is there another man?" I asked.

She went her usual shade of crimson. I thought so.

"Well, actually ..."

She hadn't strayed too far away - her latest heart-throb was a new tenor in the choir. "He's nineteen," she mooned. "His name's Stephen - isn't that a fabulous name?"

It sounded pretty ordinary to me.

"Fabulous," I said obediently.

"He stands behind me - he ties my hair to the choir stalls." It was hardly my idea of a sign of true love, but Maudie seemed happy enough with it. I couldn't understand Maudie's passions - I'm sure I'll never get like that over men.

Two things happened the next day. I developed a sore throat, and it started to rain. I didn't own up about the throat - I didn't want to be sent packing to bed while Maudie was still here. She was only staying four days and I didn't want anything to spoil it. We put mackintoshes and wellies on, and I showed her the shops and the Common, and we took a bus out to Oaklands.

"Funny it's so awful," mused Maudie, standing in the drive. "It looks gorgeous from outside."

I went to bed that night feeling quite exhausted. I'd

better be feeling all right tomorrow, I told myself. Tomorrow we were going to London Zoo with Miss Bullock and Grace.

Well, I didn't feel all right the next day. If anything, I felt worse – my throat was like sandpaper and I seemed to be aching all over. I forced myself out of bed. You'll be OK when you get there, I said firmly to myself.

The day was still grey and dismal, the roads wet and greasy-looking, but it wasn't actually raining. Miss Bullock packed sandwiches and thermoses of soup and coffee into a bag. Grace came round in Joshua's car and we went off to catch the train. The others were chattering and laughing, so luckily they didn't seem to notice I was a bit quiet.

I don't remember much about London Zoo. I seemed to be walking along in a grey cloud. As long as I keep inside this grey cloud, I told myself, hugging myself inside it, I'll be all right. I'll be able to keep going just as long as nobody tears it open.

All my limbs felt stuffed with sawdust, my head full of hot candy floss. I kept coughing; the cough wrenched at my chest. Can you have a heart attack at thirteen, I wondered. My face and body were burning with heat, my hands and feet felt icy cold. When at last it started to rain I held my roasting face up to the cooling drops. I could almost hear them sizzling as they fell on me.

All day we trudged along, through the puddles, along the paths, into the various animal houses. The only thing I remember is the smell inside the elephant house – an almost physical wall of smell, thick and hot and dark beige. It cleared my head, just for a moment.

"Are you all right, Lizzie?" Miss Bullock asked me once. I turned all my energy on.

"Yes, fine, thanks."

I suppose we must have stopped for lunch, although I can't recall eating anything.

After centuries of this, the grey cloud was beginning to get a bit patchy. I made a superhuman, marathon effort and pulled at Miss Bullock's sleeve.

"If you don't mind," I said. No voice came out. "If you don't mind," I managed to croak, "I think I'd like to go home." The three of them turned to look at me, and the last bit of the grey cloud fell away ...

As I began to fall, tumbling into the red blackness which was surrounding me, I heard my name being called by thousands of voices.

"Lizzie, Lizzie!"

The whole world was shouting my name.

It turned out I had some rare virus, whose name I can't pronounce, and was rushed into hospital. It sounds awfully impressive. But it wasn't at all impressive at the time. I woke up once and thought I was still at the zoo; then I saw all the disembodied faces floating around me and I thought I was in heaven. That thought soon went: I realised it had been a bad idea to wake up. Various needles were going into my arm and my whole body felt as though the skin had been peeled off.

Eventually I woke up properly. They fed me up, stuffed me full of drugs, and let me go home. This was after a couple of weeks, and I was still pretty groggy. I was glad to be back in my own bed. They do insist on waking you up in hospital to give you something to help you sleep, when you're already sleeping quite happily without it.

I shan't go on about my getting better, but after I'd been home about ten days I began to feel more like a person.

Miss Bullock bossily took over the nursing of the invalid, bringing me fruit juice or milk on the hour every hour, and making sure I took my pills and medicine. The medicine was awful – it tasted like bad breath. But she stood over me and made me swallow it. One afternoon I decided I wanted to play Scrabble, so Miss Bullock left the ironing and came to humour me. After she told me I'd spelt my word wrong for the fourth time, though, I got really cheesed off, and knocked the board and all the little plastic tiles flying.

"I don't want to play any more," I sulked, "it's giving me a headache."

"You're just a bad loser," she replied coolly. "It's time you had some more medicine."

"You're so bossy," I snapped. "And I don't want any more medicine. It tastes foul."

We yelled at each other for a bit, until Daddy came in from his study to find out what all the fuss was about. "I see you're feeling better, Lizzie," he said drily. I think he was a bit disappointed that Miss Bullock and I weren't getting on any better. When he'd come in on the touching little scene the other week, when Rufus had started to eat, I think he'd fondly imagined that she and I were suddenly going to be in each other's pockets. Well, we weren't. Life just isn't like that, is it?

All in all, we were all glad when I got up and about again. I did some violin practice, although Miss Bullock came into the room after an hour to stop me.

"That's enough," she said. "We don't want you overdoing things on your first day." Miss Bully, I should call her. Bossy bag.

Then, one night, I had a horrendous nightmare – I dreamt I was being chased by fearsome headless monsters and my mother was trying to save me, but she couldn't reach me.

I woke up pouring with sweat and trembling all over.

"Mummy!" I screamed. "Mummy!"

The door opened and a shadowy figure came in. In that weird half-asleepness you're in after a nightmare, I thought it *was* my mother, come to save me from the nameless terrors.

"Mummy!" I hurled myself into her arms. I realised then, of course, that it was Miss Bullock and not Mummy at all, but strangely it didn't seem to matter.

She held me and stroked my hair until the horrors subsided.

"It's all right, Lizzie – it's just a bad dream." That's what Mummy always used to say to me after nightmares.

When the bad dream had vanished, she stood up to go. I grabbed her hand.

"Don't go – I might dream it again."

Then, for some inexplicable reason, I started to cry. I sobbed and sobbed, and she held my hand all the while.

I told her everything – how I'd resented her marrying Daddy, taking him away when he'd been solely mine since Mummy died; how I hated moving away from Cornwall, to Barnes and Oaklands – awful Oaklands, with its sport, and being ignored; and Amber, and Camilla, and Ooh-aar Oliver, and the liver; and running away from the disco.

I told her about stealing money from her purse, and getting drunk at Emma's birthday party; about Ben and Maudie in the summer holidays, and being jealous; and Maudie's mother, and the row with Ben. And I told her about my fears of when the new baby came, of losing Daddy's love and being passed over.

Out it all came, in a mixed-up, unstoppable flood.

When I'd finished, she wiped my face with a hanky.

"Blow," she said. I blew. She regarded me with such a sad face, I felt like crying again.

But I don't think she was sad.

"Thank you for telling me all that," she said at last. "I'm so sorry you've had to go through it all on your own. But I guess it's all part of that rotten experience called growing up." She grimaced at me. "If it's any comfort to you," she went on, "I can promise you that the new baby won't make a scrap of difference to the way your Daddy loves you. Love's a funny thing – it has elastic sides. It's not like a cake which you have to cut up into portions to give people: a big bit for her, a little bit for him, and when it's all finished, that's it. There's always room to add something else, without the existing love diminishing in any way. Can you understand that?"

"I think so," I said. The trouble was, my elastic seemed to have perished just lately. I'd have to do something about it.

Miss Bullock went on: "Your Daddy loves you very much indeed." She lowered her voice until I could barely hear her. "And I love you, too. I know I can never be your mother, and I wouldn't try to be – I can't replace her, I know that. But what I can be is your friend. That's what I want us to be – friends."

There was a long silence. I could hear the clock ticking.

"Do you think that's possible, Lizzie?"

I looked at her for an endless moment.

"Yes," I said solemnly. "I think so."

"Good. Now try and get some sleep – and no more bad dreams."

She kissed my forehead and was gone.

9

The last Straw!

Things did improve after that – I can see that now, looking back. At the time, though, I just felt relieved at having told Miss Bullock everything. I didn't mention any of it to Daddy, though – and I didn't know whether she would or not. I rather hoped not.

I began to think of the house in Barnes as 'home', which was something I thought I'd never do. It wasn't the Cornish cottage and never would be, but it did have familiar things in it and my room was looking nice now.

While I was convalescing, Daddy brought me home a load of paint charts – cards with little squares of colour on, so you can choose the shade you like. He said I could have whatever colour I wanted, and then I could help him paint the room. I could choose a new carpet and curtains, too. I wanted something full of brightness and sunshine, so I chose shades of cream and buttermilk and pale yellow.

I'd like to be able to say that Miss Bullock and I fell on each other's necks and became the best of friends, after I'd had that nightmare and confessed everything, but I can't. As I said in the last chapter, life just isn't like that. I sometimes wish it was: things would be much easier to bear if you knew they were always going to have a happy ending, like in books.

But we did seem to be getting on better. It was as if I was looking at things from a different angle: like in the Hall of Mirrors at a fair. You look at yourself in one mirror, and you're long and thin – in another, you're short and fat, ugly and distorted. You know it's still you, but you look totally different.

I'd been looking at things through the fat and ugly mirror: now I was seeing them more through the normal one. It wasn't the situation that had changed, it was my way of perceiving it. Daddy and Miss Bullock hadn't really been shutting me out: I'd been doing that myself, by refusing to accept the situation. So I was now trying hard to accept that things were as they were, and nothing I could say or do would alter them. It wasn't easy though: it wasn't easy at all.

After I'd told Miss Bullock everything, the one thing that preyed on my mind was the money I'd stolen from her. I knew now it was stealing – I couldn't kid myself otherwise.

I also realised the reason for the stolen money still being on my mind. It was my conscience pricking me. I was amazed to find I still had a conscience – it seemed to have been in hibernation during the past few months. I decided to approach Miss Bullock about it again; when I confessed for the second time, she considered me gravely. "Do you remember how much it was, altogether?" she asked me.

"A few pounds – well, actually about twenty-five," I muttered.

Her eyebrows raised, but she made no comment on the amount. "I know," she said, after a few moments, "you can pay me back out of your pocket money – a bit each week. I don't suppose you've got twenty-five pounds saved away in a lump and, even if you have, I wouldn't want to take it away from you like that. No – you pay me, say, a pound each week. Does that sound reasonable?"

I nodded.

"Then," she went on, "I'll save it all up until you've paid back the whole amount. Then you can give it to charity – that way, you've paid back the money and it's gone somewhere useful." It sounded like a good idea to me: I decided to send the money to the RSPCA. My conscience was salved, although I swore I'd never steal anything ever again.

Things at home may have quietened down, but things at school were soon back to normal. Awful, I mean. I didn't go back until the beginning of December. I'd been off for five weeks and only went back then because I was getting so bored at home. The doctor said it wouldn't hurt me, as there were only three weeks of the term left until we broke up for Christmas.

It did hurt me, though. All the time I was sitting at home, getting more and more fed up with the endless games of Monopoly and Scrabble, the jigsaws that always had a crucial bit missing, the books I'd read a hundred times before and hadn't even enjoyed the first time – all this time, I was thinking about going back to school and looking forward to it. Looking forward to it! – I must have been bonkers. It's odd how your mind can play funny tricks, assuring you that any situation is better than the one you're in.

Once I got back to Oaklands, of course, I wished I was back at home in Barnes, reading *The Hobbit* for the umpteenth time. Even the novelty of having been so ill, and telling everybody about it, wore off during the first morning. Amber started her tricks again – my pen and ruler disappeared during Geography – and I tried to convince her I was still contagious. Infectious, I mean.

"You can't be," she said loftily, "or you wouldn't have been allowed back to school."

Not only did I have Amber Delaney to contend with again, but I seemed to have fallen such a long way behind in the work. The five weeks I'd missed seemed like five terms, especially in Maths. I felt a bit worried. I was in the third year now: after Christmas, we were supposed to be starting to choose the subjects we wanted to take for GCSE. I didn't have a clue what I wanted to study. It would be easier, I reflected, if I could say what subjects I *didn't* want to do: the only trouble with that being, I'd only end up with Music and perhaps French. I didn't think they'd let me do only two subjects. Apart from anything else, we all had to do Maths and English, one language and one science. English and the language were all right – but the thought of taking Maths filled me with horror. I'd spent all the previous year in Cornwall playing Battleships with Maudie during Maths lessons – the teacher wasn't very observant – and I'd managed to scrape through the last term-and-a-bit at Oaklands by pretending I wasn't used to the method they taught. But I couldn't get away with that for much longer.

So far as choosing the science was concerned, I could see myself resorting to the pin method: I was equally hopeless in all three, Physics, Chemistry and Biology. I'll never forget the Biology teacher asking me what the Latin name for rabbit was, and me saying Bunnius. I thought it was an inspired guess. The teacher thought I was being cheeky.

What with worrying about all this, and Amber starting off again, I was exhausted at the end of my first day. Daddy had said *he* would pick me up as I'd been ill. As I walked out of the school gates I passed Amber. She and Camilla were standing on the corner amid a crowd of boys, smoking. I had to admire their nerve: they could easily be seen from the staff room and smoking was considered the Eighth Deadly Sin at Oaklands.

I heard Amber's clear, upper-class voice ring out. "Look," she drawled, "it's Ooh-aar Oliver." She lazily detached herself from the crowd and sauntered over towards me, hands on hips. "Where are you going?" she demanded, blocking my path. "Why aren't you getting the bus?"

"My father's come to collect me," I replied calmly. "Get out of my way, please."

To my surprise, she moved aside immediately. But she hadn't finished with me.

"Poor little baby," she jeered softly. "Oo's got 'er Daddy to come and collect 'er, then? Diddums!"

I got into the car, glad to escape her mocking voice.

"Hello, Daddy," I said. "Hello, Miss Bullock." She was there too.

"Who's that?" Daddy asked, as we drove past Amber.

"That's Amber Delaney," I said. My eyes met Miss Bullock's in the mirror.

"Sixth former?" she asked casually, although she knew otherwise.

"No – she's in my class."

"Good Lord," said Daddy. "Thirteen going on twenty-five, eh? I wonder if her parents know she smokes."

"I somehow doubt it," said Miss Bullock drily. She grinned at me suddenly in the driving mirror. "Did you have a good day, Lizzie?"

"It wasn't too bad," I replied.

Amber stepped up her 'I hate Lizzie Oliver' campaign with a vengeance – and there was I, just before half-term, thinking she'd got bored with it and stopped. I rang Maudie one evening to have a moan.

"What on earth shall I do?" I asked my friend. "She's making my life a misery."

"Poor you," Maudie sympathised. "I don't suppose you can try the liver trick again, can you?"

"Not really – it was good the first time, but I don't think she'll fall for it again."

"Not even if you do a variation – put it in the bottom of her bag this time, instead of her lunchbox. Something like that."

I considered it.

"No," I said, "I really don't think it would work."

"Well," said Maudie, "I think you'll just have to try and ignore her – rise above her."

"I do try," I sighed, "but it's ever so difficult. I'm fed up with my belongings vanishing, too – it's costing me a fortune in pens and things."

"She'll get fed up eventually," Maudie assured me. "Bullies always do. Look at how those boys were with me when I first started here. I just ignored them until they gave up."

I hadn't realised she'd been purposely ignoring them – I'd thought she was too wet to stand up for herself. My friend Maudie was full of surprises.

"How's – um – whatsisname?" I couldn't remember Maudie's heart-throb's name.

She pretended she couldn't remember it either, for a moment. "Do you mean Stephen?" she said off-handedly.

"Och, I couldn't care less. I'm off men."

It transpired he'd started going out with Beth – Beth from the church choir, who was only a year or so older than us. Poor Maudie – "I'm doomed to be unlucky in love," she said gloomily. Then Daddy started making a loud fuss about the phone bill, so I had to ring off. But talking to Maudie had cheered me up a bit, even though the problem with Amber Delaney was still there to be solved.

The first week back, she was worse than ever. It finally came to a head on the Friday, though not the sort of head I had anticipated. On this particular Friday, I'd eaten my lunch and was walking across the playground, carrying my violin, *en route* to the music room. Suddenly, Amber Delaney was in front of me.

"Where are you off to?" she sneered. She seemed to have grown since I'd been ill – either that or I'd shrunk. Even allowing for the three-inch heels she wore, flouting school rules *and* getting away with it as usual, she was a good six inches taller than me.

"I'm going to Orchestra," I said – politely, I thought, under the circumstances. "Will you move, please – I'm going to be late."

She laughed nastily. The three or four Mafioso she always had with her laughed too, like the parrots they were. "So what?" she said. "So what if you are late? You won't get told off – you're Miss Berkowitz's pet."

"Teacher's pet," said one of the parrots.

"Teacher's pet," one of the others repeated wittily.

"Amber," I said patiently, "get out of the way."

"I don't want to," she said. "I want to teach you some manners – some respect for your betters."

I laughed – I couldn't help it. "Oh yes," I said

sarcastically, "so you think you're better than me?"

Amber's face darkened with temper. She looked me up and down, looking for something else about me to mock, and her glance fell on my violin. She looked up again, into my face, and smiled evilly. Then she made a grab for the violin case. I tried not to let go, but didn't have much chance – the parrots were hanging onto me, holding me back.

"Leave that alone!" I shouted. "Don't you dare touch my violin!"

I struggled and the parrots increased their grip. There were four of them and only one of me – I might as well have stood still for all the good it did.

Amber's mighty brain finally worked out how to open the locks on the heavy, rectangular violin case. She placed it on the ground and surveyed the contents for a moment, then she took the violin out.

"No!" I shrieked. "No! Leave it alone, you horrible ..." I couldn't think of a word strong enough.

Amber realised that smashing the violin would have been going it a bit: half the school seemed to be crowding around, drawn by my screams, as people always are by the prospect of drama. There were too many witnesses. Amber put the violin down and I sighed with relief. Then her hands appeared again over the open lid of the case, like a conjurer drawing a rabbit from a hat: only what she had in her hands was not a rabbit but my violin bow.

She held it in her right hand like a whip. She straightened up and came over to me. Then she hit me across the face with it, twice, once on either cheek.

It stung like mad and brought tears to my eyes. But that was nothing compared to what I felt when I saw what she did next. She held the bow with a hand at either end, then quite deliberately brought it down over her knee – and snapped it in two. The horsehair dangled uselessly from the broken sticks.

I saw red – I literally had a red haze in front of my eyes. Howling with rage, I heaved myself away from my goggle-eyed captors and flung myself at Amber.

I pulled her hair. I scratched her face. I ripped her jersey. I bit her hand as she tried to restrain me. We fell on the ground, and as we rolled around on the dusty tarmac I fought and bit and kicked and scratched, and all the while I heard this weird high-pitched noise.

Eventually, a teacher came and pulled us apart – Mrs Fotherington, the games teacher. The noise stopped: I realised it had been me, screaming.

Mrs Fotherington marched us both by the scruff of our necks to the school office, deposited us there and went in to see the Headmistress. The school secretary made us sit in opposite corners of the room – she looked afraid that we might start fighting again, and she didn't look capable of separating an egg, let alone two scrapping, strapping teenage girls.

I looked at Amber and she looked at me. She'd definitely come off worse. Her blonde hair was muddied and tangled, her jersey ripped from hem to neck. Her face had a scarlet weal above her right eyebrow and one of her three-inch heels had snapped off. Her lower lip was cut and swollen.

I was a bit dusty, and red in the face. My knees were cut, where I'd hurled myself at her in the rugby tackle Ben had taught me a year ago. My elbow ached where I'd fallen on it. But I was elated and punchdrunk, and triumphant. I'd beaten Amber Delaney and she knew it.

She dissolved into noisy tears as the door opened and Miss Carrington-Smythe came in.

10

An End — and a new Beginning

I didn't stay feeling triumphant for long. To my utter amazement, Miss Carrington-Smythe rounded on *me*: it was obvious she thought it was all my fault.

She ushered us into her office, bootfaced. "Sit down, dear," she said to Amber, who was sobbing pitifully. "Not you," she snapped at me as I went to sit down too. "You can stand – here, in front of me, where I can see you."

I duly stood there, hands behind my back. I lifted my chin defiantly – I wasn't ashamed. I had only given Amber what she'd had coming to her for ages.

"Now then," said Miss Carrington-Smythe to Amber, "tell me what happened. Gently now – take your time," as a fresh burst of sobbing came from the blonde girl.

I was disgusted with her – I knew she was putting it on for the Headmistress's benefit, and more than likely to give herself time to make up some pack of lies to explain herself away.

Sure enough, after a few moments Amber's flood dried up. That's when I was certain she'd been putting it on: as she raised her head there wasn't a tear to be seen. No red eyes, no swollen red cheeks – nothing. You ratbag, I thought.

"Oh, Miss Carrington-Smythe," she said in a small voice, "it was awful. She'd dropped her violin – I was just giving it back to her and she simply turned on me. She was like an animal – it was awful," she repeated, giving a theatrical shudder and manufacturing another sob.

I couldn't believe she had the nerve – there must have been at least twenty girls standing around us, witnesses to her real actions.

"She's a liar," I burst out, "she took my violin and broke my bow – ask anyone. Ask – ask Sophie Smith." I'd noticed Harriet's middle sister amongst the crowd of onlookers.

"That's enough," the Headmistress boomed. "I am quite capable of forming my own opinions without the need to consult any of your 'friends'." She put inverted commas around the word, distastefully.

"But she did," I said frantically, "she *did*! She broke it – I'll show you." I didn't know what had happened to the violin and broken bow – still sitting in the middle of the playground for all I knew. But when I found it I could show Miss Carrington-Smythe the evidence – she'd have to believe me then.

"Little gel," said the Headmistress sternly, "are you questioning my judgement?"

I couldn't see what judgement had to do with it. I knew I was speaking the truth: I had been there. She hadn't. "You don't understand ..." I began to protest.

"I understand perfectly. I have had unsatisfactory reports about you since you started at Oaklands. Now this has happened. You have introduced an undesirable element into the school and I intend to eradicate it. Do you hear me? – eradicate it!" Her voice rose alarmingly.

I shot a look at Amber. She sat there smugly, a self-satisfied smirk on her face. My heart sank at the

Headmistress's next words.

"I wish to see your parents about this," she said. "You can tell them what has happened and I shall write to them this very afternoon. They may telephone me to make an appointment. Is that clear?" she demanded. I nodded, dumbfounded.

"I'm afraid I shall have to ask your mother to come along, too, dear," she informed Amber, her tone changing to sweetness and light. "You do understand, don't you?"

"Yes, Miss Carrington-Smythe," answered Amber demurely, eyes downcast. "I don't know what Mummy and Daddy will have to say about me being beaten up, though – at Oaklands, of all places!"

This seemed to worry Miss Carrington-Smythe: I couldn't understand why. "I'm sure we'll be able to reassure them that it was an unusual occurrence – most unlikely to happen again," she said hastily.

"I hope so, Miss Carrington-Smythe," said Amber, still the model of innocence.

The Headmistress turned back to me. "I take a dim view of this – very dim indeed. I will see to it that you are punished accordingly: you have my assurance of that. I will not have my gels fighting like guttersnipes." She dismissed me with an imperious wave of her hand. "Shut the door behind you."

As I went out, I heard her say to Amber, "Would you like a nice lie-down in the Medical Room for the rest of the afternoon, dear?" I was stunned by the injustice of it.

I didn't dare tell Daddy about it when I got home. What would he say about me fighting in the playground "like a guttersnipe"? Although I knew I was in the right, I feared he might take Miss Carrington-Smythe's view of the matter – that it was all my fault. Still, I had to tell him my side of it before the Headmistress's letter arrived on Monday, or even tomorrow: I grew alarmed at the prospect. It all depended on when the old bag posted it. If she managed to catch Friday's last post, I only had that evening to pluck up the courage to tell Daddy.

I couldn't concentrate on my violin lesson that evening. My mind kept wandering – it was most unlike me. I was so worried about what would happen at school. There was also the matter of the broken bow. Luckily, it was only my second-best bow – the best one was still in the case, unharmed, and I was using that. But the broken one was in my case – I hadn't dared to leave it behind, even in my bedroom. Somebody would have been bound to find it: Rufus, probably, thinking it was a new toy and taking it downstairs to show everybody. He wasn't called a retriever for nothing. And I couldn't throw the bow away – it was my evidence, so I left it in the case, and at my lesson I managed to get my stuff out of the case without Mr Owen noticing the broken bow.

Halfway through the lesson, a string broke. I went to my case to get another one and, before I could stop him, Mr Owen crossed the room and was standing over me. He couldn't help but notice the broken bow.

"Dear oh dear," he said, picking it up. "What a lovely mess!"

I silently changed my violin string. Mr Owen thoughtfully weighed the bow in his hands.

"Is this why you've been so distracted today? You haven't told your Dad about the bow?" It would have been easier to say 'Yes' – after all, it was partly true. But I didn't.

"Not exactly," I said.

"What's the problem, then?" His lovely Welsh voice

was gentle and understanding.

The temptation was too great. "Can you keep a secret?" I asked him.

I told him about the fight and everything. He was very sympathetic.

"If I were you," he said when I'd finished, "I'd tell your Dad as soon as you get home."

"I know I should," I sighed, "but he'll be furious – I know he will. And then there's the broken bow. He'll be hopping mad." I lapsed into gloomy silence.

"Try it," advised Mr Owen confidently, "you may be pleasantly surprised at his reaction." It sounded doubtful to me – after all, Mr Owen had only met Daddy a couple of times, so he hardly knew him – but he was convinced I should tell Daddy as soon as I got home. So, knees knocking and heart pounding, I did. I finished up by telling him about Miss Carrington-Smythe's summons to go and see her.

Mr Owen was wrong. I wasn't surprised at Daddy's reaction – I was flabbergasted. When I told him about the broken bow he went red with anger, as I knew he would. But when I got to the bit about me rugby-tackling Amber and then us rolling around fighting on the ground, he let out a great whoop.

Then I realised he was laughing – although laughing is hardly a descriptive enough word for the noise he was making. He rolled around on the sofa, clutching his sides, his eyes streaming. I was a bit worried – I thought he'd flipped. I couldn't see what there was to laugh about. Neither could Miss Bullock – she sat there, tight-lipped, not saying a word.

At last, he stopped. He wiped his eyes with his hanky and blew his nose. "Oh, Lizzie," he said weakly, "I wish

I'd been there to see that little madam get her come-
uppance. You should have blacked her eye for her!"

"Jamie!" said Miss Bullock, shocked.

"Well, she should have," said Daddy, unrepentant.
"*You* weren't hurt, were you, sweetie?" he asked me
anxiously.

"Of course I wasn't," I said boastfully. "I'm much
stronger than her - I hate to think what she'd have
ended up looking like if Mrs Fotherington hadn't come
along and split us up."

Daddy chuckled. "I suppose I'll have to go along and
butter Miss Carrington-Thing up, all the same."

Miss Bullock was outraged. "Certainly not!" she cried.
"Poor Lizzie's had to put up with this Amber creature for
weeks and you talk about buttering the old crow up?" I
was even more surprised at this than I had been at
Daddy's reaction.

"I didn't mean that," said Daddy gently. "Of course I
know Lizzie's in the right - the bow business was
obviously the last straw for her." I nodded: I still couldn't
believe their reaction. "But I don't see what good it will
do if I go along and sound off. She'll only take it out on
Lizzie in the long run. That type always do," he added
darkly.

"Let *me* go, then," Miss Bullock said unexpectedly.
"Please, Jamie - I know how to deal with that sort of
head teacher. The one at my last school but one was like
it - you just play them at their own game."

Daddy looked doubtful. "I don't know ..."

Miss Bullock turned to me. "Would you mind if I
went, Lizzie, instead of your father?"

"I don't mind," I said honestly. "I wish neither of you
had to, really." On balance, I thought I'd probably prefer
her - I didn't want Daddy crawling to Miss Carrington-

Smythe, and the alternative was that he'd lose his temper. At least Miss Bullock had experience of dealing with this sort of thing – confronting irate headmistresses, I mean.

So it was that Miss Bullock arrived at Oaklands just before the appointed time of ten o'clock on Tuesday morning. Miss Carrington-Smythe wanted me there too – I hadn't expected that, and felt very nervous waiting outside her door for the royal command, "Enter." Miss Bullock squeezed my shoulder.

"Don't worry!" she whispered. "We'll win!" She was dressed in a navy-blue suit, and looked very smart and businesslike.

Amber was already in the Headmistress's office, with a woman I would have recognised anywhere as her mother. She was a larger, blonder, heavily made-up version of Amber herself. She was wearing a stupid hat with a large bird's feather shoved through it and was holding a teacup with her little finger delicately crooked. Amber sniggered as we entered the room.

Miss Carrington-Smythe looked up at us over the top of her pince-nez. Her features hardened as she saw Miss Bullock.

"Oh," she said, giving the word two syllables. "I was expecting one of Elizabeth's parents. Who might you be, young lady – her sister? It really won't do, you know. It was to her parents I wrote."

Miss Bullock drew herself up to her full height, which wasn't very much. It looked impressive, though.

"I," she said frostily, "am Elizabeth's stepmother. I should be grateful if you would address me as Mrs Oliver."

That threw the Headmistress off-guard for a moment.

"I do apologise, Mrs Oliver," she said, recovering. "Let me introduce Mrs Delaney – her husband is the chairman of the board of governors, you know – and this is her daughter, Amber." Miss Bullock's eyebrows disappeared into her hairline.

"Really?" she drawled. "The *chairman*? How very interesting."

That explained Miss Carrington-Smythe's willingness to accept Amber's side of the story and not mine, I thought. I was filled with dismay. I knew we'd never win now.

But I was wrong. Miss Bullock was magnificent – she didn't let the Headmistress get a word in edgeways. She went on about how disgusted she and "Elizabeth's father" were with the continual bullying "Elizabeth" had had to put up with since starting at Oaklands. Miss Bullock went on about how disappointed they were that Oaklands seemed incapable of monitoring such bullying and putting an end to it; and that they were unhappy with my lack of progress there, "due," she said, "to being under-stimulated mentally. Also," she said, "there is the small matter of the broken bow." She produced the pieces from her handbag with a flourish.

Miss Carrington-Smythe began to protest, weakly. "Amber says Elizabeth broke it herself to lend credence to her story ..."

Miss Bullock laughed shortly.

"Really," she said. "That bow cost eighty-five pounds – I don't really think my step-daughter would indulge in that kind of vandalism simply to prove her point – bear in mind she is a violinist, with respect for all things concerning the violin." I hardly recognised myself from these descriptions.

"She did break it herself!" cried Amber shrilly. "She

did! *She's* the liar – she just wanted to get me into trouble!" I was furious.

"What about the girls who saw Amber do it?" I remembered suddenly, turning to the Headmistress.

"Have you asked any of them about the incident?" asked Miss Bullock softly.

There was a nasty pause. Then: "We'll send you a cheque," Mrs Delaney burst out. It was the first thing she'd said. "Eighty-five pounds, didn't you say?"

Miss Bullock nodded. "Thank you," she said graciously.

Miss Carrington-Smythe tried once more. "There is still the fighting," she said. "I simply cannot allow my gels to ..."

"You won't have to," said Miss Bullock. "My husband and I are removing Elizabeth from this school at once. It's clear that Oaklands has nothing to offer anyone with talent." And with that as her parting shot she grasped me by the hand and pulled me, dumbfounded, to the door. "I wish you all good day."

As a *pièce-de-resistance*, it couldn't have been bettered. I saw my utter astonishment mirrored on the faces of the Headmistress, Amber and Mrs Delaney, as Miss Bullock whisked me from the room.

I didn't know what to think. When we got home, Miss Bullock took off her hat and threw it onto the sofa. Then she called Daddy from his study.

"It all started when you were ill," he said. "We'd been worried about you for ages – you seemed so withdrawn. You never told us how you were settling down at Oaklands, and you kept rushing off on your own for hours on end."

"When you went into hospital," Miss Bullock went on,

"Maudie told us all about you hating Oaklands. She told us about Amber, too – she was concerned about you, you see. Then when you yourself told me how unhappy you were, we knew it was really serious and that we *had* to do something."

Daddy then told me that Miss Berkowitz and Mr Owen had written to him, quite separately, stating their concern that I wasn't getting "adequate all-round musical stimulus," as Daddy put it.

"Miss Berkowitz in particular was most anti-Oaklands," he said. "Though in actual fact, she did say that an ordinary school wasn't the best place for you anyway. Then Mr Owen wrote, telling us about this place where he teaches."

I goggled at Daddy. "The Central London School of Music?"

"That's the one," he said. "I made some enquiries, and it seems they take new pupils in January as well as September."

I could hardly believe what I was hearing. "You mean …?"

"Yes," said Miss Bullock, "you've got an audition next week. The letter came this morning. You've left Oaklands for good!"

For the next week I did nothing but music. I practised my violin until my fingers were sore, and I played the piano more than ever before, so that I could eventually do a passable rendition of a Beethoven sonata.

Miss Bullock coached me with the music theory. At first, I didn't want her help, thinking she was patronising me. But she insisted. She was very good, if something of a slave-driver. I'd forgotten she had trained to be a singer before deciding to be a teacher instead. She knew what she was talking about and it helped me enormously.

The night before the audition, I couldn't get to sleep – although I'd been exhausted during the evening and had gone to bed early. I went downstairs to get a glass of milk. Daddy was sitting at the kitchen table, checking the proofs of his latest book, so we sat and chatted.

It was a lovely cosy chat – just like the old days, when it was just the two of us. Daddy was sad that I hadn't told him how miserable I'd been at Oaklands. "If only you'd said something earlier – we'd have taken you away immediately."

"I knew Miss Bullock wanted me to go there," I explained. "I didn't think she'd want me to leave."

Daddy stared at me, perplexed. "What do you mean? *I* chose Oaklands – I'd heard it was such a good school. It has excellent exam results, and my publisher's daughter went there, apparently. She loved it – mind you, she was very sporty." He ruffled my hair, like he used to do. "Don't worry," he said, "you won't ever have to go back there."

A sudden thought occurred to me. "What if I don't get in?" I asked fearfully. "What if I fail my audition?"

"You won't," said Daddy confidently. "Have faith in yourself – everybody else knows you can do it. Now *you've* got to believe it."

The next morning I felt so nervous I couldn't eat much breakfast. I managed to force down half a cup of tea and about three Rice Krispies. Then Daddy and Miss Bullock drove me to my audition – to my doom, it felt like. As we pulled up outside the red brick Victorian building, I felt a moment of terror. I didn't want to go in. Then I forced my legs to move. I got out of the car.

"Are you sure you don't want us to come in with

you?" asked Daddy anxiously, winding down the window.

"No," I said, my voice trembling. "I'll be all right."

"Good luck, then," he said. He kissed my cheek through the open window. "We'll pick you up about twelve thirty." That was the time the letter had said the audition would finish. It was now five to ten – five minutes to go.

"Lizzie!" Miss Bullock called to me.

I looked through Daddy's window at her. "Yes?"

"Shall we go to McDonald's for lunch?" My stomach turned over at the thought of hamburgers.

"OK," I said. "See you later."

I picked up my violin and music-case, and went into the Central London School of Music.

The written paper wasn't too bad – I was very glad that Miss Bullock had crammed all those extra facts into me, though. I finished with only five minutes to spare. I threw down my pen and looked at the other candidates. There were ten of us altogether and only one boy looked about the same age as me. The others were a couple of years older.

After the paper, we had a break for orange squash and biscuits. My appetite had returned – I picked up four biscuits and wandered over to read the notices on the noticeboard.

"Hello," said a voice behind me. "What's your name?" I turned round. It was the boy from the exam – he looked nice, I decided. He had soft pale hair and bright blue eyes, and was smiling in a friendly way.

I smiled back. "Hello," I said, "I'm Lizzie Oliver. What's your name?"

"Simon," he said, "Simon Alexander. Wasn't that paper ghastly?"

"It was a bit," I agreed. "Never mind – it's over now. What's your instrument?" I asked him.

"Cello," he replied. "What do you play?"

"I'm a violinist."

At that moment, a kind-looking lady with faded grey hair pulled into a bun came into the room and clapped her hands for silence. "The audition panel has drawn the order for you to play. The first person they would like to hear is," she looked at the list in her hand, "Elizabeth Oliver."

"What luck!" Simon whispered to me, "I wish *I* could go first."

"If the rest of you would like to go to the Common Room to wait," the lady went on, "I'll call you in turn."

Everyone trooped off. "Good luck," said one or two to me as they passed. Simon crossed his fingers at me. The bun lady ushered me into a large room.

There were four people seated behind a long table, each with a blotter and a glass of water before him.

There was a fierce-looking man with iron-grey hair and horn-rimmed spectacles. Next to him was a dark, gypsy-like lady with square-cut hair, like Miss Bullock's, and a square neckline to match. She was the only one who smiled at me as I entered the room. Sitting next to her was a youngish man who looked frightened, like a fawn. His tie and shirt and jacket all clashed and I could see, under the table, that he was wearing odd socks. Finally, at the end of the table, there was a hugely fat man with a red face like a squashed tomato. He had bushy grey eyebrows and looked as though he was asleep.

"Hello, Elizabeth," the fierce man greeted me.

"Oh, please," I said, more boldly than I felt, "please call

me Lizzie – everybody does. I hate being called Elizabeth." Mr Fierce raised an eyebrow. The gypsy lady's smile became even broader.

"Very well," said Mr Fierce. "Allow me to introduce the audition panel. I am Mr Bishop, the Musical Director of the school." He indicated the gypsy lady. "This is Miss Quentin – she is in charge of the string teaching."

She smiled at me again. "Hello, Lizzie."

Mr Fierce – I mean Mr Bishop – introduced the other two. The fawn, Mr Blenkinsop, blushed and dropped his pencil. The squashed tomato's name was Signor Sporanti. He was Italian. He grunted and went back to sleep.

I played my two violin pieces – an unaccompanied Bach Partita, or rather part of it, and a dashing gypsyish piece by Ravel, called *Tzigane* – rather well, I thought. Miss Quentin sat very still on the edge of her chair whilst I played. Then she wrote frantically on her blotter, biting her underlip. The panel all looked at each other.

"Thank you," said Mr Bishop gravely. "Now will you play your piano piece, please."

The accompanist got up from the piano stool and left the room. I sat down nervously. I was regretting my choice of Beethoven sonata. Then, suddenly, I had a brainwave.

"I'm very sorry," I said, "but I've forgotten to bring my music. Do you mind if I play something else, instead?"

"I suppose not," said Mr Bishop. "What will you play instead?"

"It's called *Improvisation*," I said, "by Lizzie Oliver."

And I played about Penwithin, and the Strand, and the cliffs, and Penlorren, and the seagulls. Everything I loved about Cornwall came through my fingers and onto the keys, and for a while I forgot I was in this room, being auditioned, and I lost myself in the music.

As the last chords died away, I came back to earth. I met Miss Quentin's eyes and we stared at each other for a long moment. Then she started to clap. Mr Bishop and Mr Blenkinsop joined in. Only Signor Sporanti dozed on in the corner.

The rest of the audition went by in a flash. At last, it was over. The 'viva' was very brief. They just asked me how long I'd been playing, and a bit about my other school work, and who my instrument teachers were. When I told them I'd taught myself the piano, mostly at any rate, after three years of deadly dull lessons in Penwithin, they muttered amongst themselves. I was cross with myself – that was obviously the wrong answer.

"Thank you, Lizzie," said Mr Bishop eventually. "We'll let you know as soon as possible."

It was a dismissal, but I couldn't go. I simply couldn't move.

"Is there anything wrong?" he asked.

"Please," I said breathlessly. I couldn't stand the thought of having to wait to find out whether I'd got in or not. "Please – can't you tell me *now*? Please – I know you shouldn't, but I simply can't bear not knowing."

That woke up even Signor Sporanti. He blinked in amazement. "What ees?" he demanded. "She wanna know now? OK – you tell her now."

Mr Bishop and the other two exchanged glances.

"Very well," said Mr Bishop. "Although it's highly irregular, I can tell you that we're very pleased to be able to offer you a place, beginning in January."

I whooped with joy – I couldn't help it. "Oh, thank you, thank you," I squeaked.

Miss Quentin beamed at me. "May I ask you

something?" she said. "What were you thinking about when you were improvising on the piano just now?" I told her the truth.

"My real home," I said. "Cornwall."

I walked out on air. Miss Bullock was waiting for me in the vast marble hall, pacing up and down anxiously. When she saw me she hurried over.

"Where's Daddy?" I asked, containing myself.

"He's been held up," she said. "He'll meet us in McDonald's. Well – how did it go?"

I couldn't stay calm any longer. I leapt up and down on the steps: I could hardly speak, I was so happy.

"I got in," I said finally. "They've given me a place!"

Miss Bullock flung her arms round me and we stood there on the steps, hugging each other, laughing and crying at the same time. We must have looked a right pair.

At last, she disentangled herself. Her make-up was smudged – either by her happy-tears or mine, I couldn't tell.

"Lizzie," she said softly, "I'm so proud of you."

I looked suitably modest. Then my tummy rumbled noisily and I remembered I'd had no breakfast.

"I'm starving," I said, taking her hand and dragging her down the steps. "Come on, Wendy – let's go and find Daddy!"

About this Author

Catherine Robinson has been writing stories since the age of seven. The idea for Lizzie Oliver came to her while in the bath – and she was inspired to search out the diaries of her own childhood. The things which are important to Lizzie, her family, friends, music and pets, reflect the author's own concerns at Lizzie's age. But Lizzie's account is also a true picture of what it's like to grow up today.

Mrs Robinson lives in North Wales with her husband, dog, and Fishpaste, the cat. This is her first novel.